THE JAMES GANG

Tim Donahue

CENTRAL PARK SOUTH PUBLISHING

Published by Central Park South Publishing 2023
www.centralparksouthpublishing.com

Typesetting and e-book formatting services by Victor Marcos

ISBN:
978-1-956452-48-8 (pbk)
978-1-956452-49-5 (hbk)
978-1-956452-50-1 (ebk)

✑1999✑

Glenn James thumbed at a script from the fourth season of *The James Gang* until the paper's white pulp ground into a soggy gray color that combined with the leftover dirt that snuck onto her fingertips. She didn't watch as she dog-eared every corner of every page that she mindlessly flipped through while her eyes focused away from her hands. She didn't even notice the small paper cut that had formed within the web-like skin that stretched between her index-finger and thumb. Her mind was too focused on the one that stood before her.

Glenn James had been the apple of her father's eye since birth. Born for stardom, her father sometimes bragged that she came out of the womb with a hand already planted in the cement of the Hollywood Walk of Fame. Her willowy hands matched a willowy person whose long arms and legs had to fold themselves into very acute angles to fit on the small sofa that her father had placed when he purchased their mansion. And while slenderness is often mistaken for elegance in places where the shoe doesn't fit, Glenn James never failed to live up to her royalty.

If appearances told all, Glenn James would have been a real chore to talk to. Her sheer slender form allowed little space for a brain of any real mass, yet her attention was completely captured by the man that stood on the other side of the foyer. His name was Hersey James.

"I just want you to know that no matter how far off my travels may take me, how many people I get to see and how much of the world I get to experience... I will always find my home inside the arms of the ones I love the most... My family." A tear beaded around the corner of Hersey James's red left eye. He held his breath for a moment, as if he were waiting for some kind of answer. His tear slid along the lines that time had worn into his face, and he blinked it away with a smile. "Scene!"

"Bravo!" Glenn sprung from her uncomfortable seat on the couch with a flurry of applause. She wrapped the old man into a hug before repelling just enough to speak without drowning her voice in his shoulder. "You haven't lost a step, it was just like the old *James Gang*!"

Hersey placed a wrinkling, reddening hand around his daughter's upper-arm—the arm that hadn't wrapped quite as tight around his neck—and pulled her away from him with a motion that flung Glenn back down into the tiny sofa.

Everlasting in her smile, Glenn watched with great expectation while Hersey sat down across from her in a seat that matched Glenn's in both pattern and color. Hersey's monochrome wardrobe was navy blue from his boat shoes to his raincoat, and all the way up to his trusty navy blue beret. Though this outfit gave him the appearance of a real snob against the zany backdrop of the polka-dotted chair, he rarely changed out of his blue uniform. In fact, ever since his best-friend William Elliott died in a bungee-jumping accident in the summer of 1996, nobody had ever seen him take off those navy blue boat shoes.

This particular outfit had become such a habit for Hersey that Glenn didn't even notice it as a peculiarity in her young life. It was merely a fact of living in the mansion that *The James Gang* built.

Hersey let out a filtered kind of sigh when he sat down. He didn't make much sound, but it was enough to prompt his daughter into a look of alarm. "What's wrong?" Glenn frowned, but her forehead refused to show any kinds of lines that would indicate her confusion. Hersey paused for a minute before finally, painstakingly, he conjured enough strength to speak.

"I just..." Hersey James bit his fist and swallowed hard before regaining his ability to speak. "I just wish the rest of The James Gang was still around to perform these lines with me!" Glenn's father barely managed to get those last words out before burying his red eyes into the palms of his hands.

Glenn was quick to place a hand on top of her father's cowering back. She peeled the corners of her long, leaf-like lips into the shape of a sympathetic smile. She rubbed small circles along the shoulderblades of Hersey's dry raincoat. She bit her lip for a moment before daring to ask the question that had swam to the front of what was usually such a selfless mind.

"What do you mean?" Hersey—expecting sweet affirmations when he received that question—lifted his head away from its resignation to his palms.

"What do you mean, what do I mean?" He barked in a voice that had lost its sense of helplessness. Hersey frowned in the face of his youngest daughter, disappointment drained from his red eyes along with whatever tears had lingered from his stage cry just moments ago.

"Well…" Glenn's words poured out like the thickest of liquids, she was being very deliberate about which ones she should pick next. "I am right here." She said, and Hersey stood up with a huff of air that billowed up from the deepest crevice of his chest. He scowled at his youngest daughter as she forced herself to retain a smile that had turned awkward when confronted by her father's over seriousness.

"Oh, you know it's not the same!" Hersey said, speaking through the filter of his mustache. His voice provided Glenn with the same unease that she would have had, had she been having this conversation with a ventriloquist. "You weren't even on the show until the last season!" Hersey scowled at his daughter. In his mind, the depravity of a life that hadn't begun and ended with the adventure show that defined the 1970s was a sin so unforgivable that the mere nature of this conversation was enough to bewilder him.

"I was on the season that you were reciting from. I was there when you said those lines!" Glenn attempted to defend herself, though she was still smiling in between her words. Thus was her nature. "I was America's sweetheart! You used to say it yourself, don't you remember?"

"It's not the same. You were a baby, you never got to be a part of that family. Not like you should have, at least." Hersey seemed to be calming down, he folded his arms and scrunched his navy blue raincoat into bunches around his elbows. His gaze veered to Glenn's left as the two of them settled into uncomfortable silence. Glenn was secretly thankful that Hersey had started to direct his bitter focus onto something other than her. Still, she couldn't help herself from breaking the silence.

"What're you looking at?" Historically, Glenn James had always been an enemy of silence; it crept in and crawled around in her gut like a parasite that could only be exercised through speech. It whispered things into her ears that she didn't want to hear. Silence was sneaky and hateful and everything else that she had spent her life in stark opposition against. Glenn preferred the noise, no matter how accusatory it could be.

"Nothing." Hersey's wandering eyes had settled towards the window next to Glenn. Gazing beyond the glass, Hersey looked to the snaking driveway that housed his two cars; a cream colored Jaguar XJS from 1975, and a baby blue Dodge Challenger from 1977. "I think I'm gonna go for a drive. Which car should I take?"

"You haven't driven either of those cars in decades. I don't think I've even seen either of them run since Kitty stole the old Challenger to drive it to her prom." Glenn laughed at the memory. Her words dumped water on her father's short-lived excitement, but her smile was soft when she spoke and her breath would have tasted like strawberries if she ever let anyone close enough to taste it.

"Don't say her name around me anymore, you know I don't like that." Hersey stood up. With eyes still transfixed on the window, he tugged at the sleeves of his raincoat and walked by Glenn's seat. All Glenn could do was pivot to watch while her elderly father marched down the red marble staircase. He disappeared from her view, presumably, off to the garage en route to the driveway en route to the speeding highways that he hadn't dared to venture towards in years.

Glenn lifted herself from the seat, she climbed over a dark oak footstool that connected her chair to the foyer's coffee table that sat in front of the window that her father had just focused so intently on. Glenn was wearing a long, ivory colored gown that draped below her as she leaned over the coffee table in order to gain a better view out the window. There her father sat, straight-backed in the driver's seat of his once glamorous Jaguar XJS. There, he prepared to wow his youngest and most agreeable daughter as he snapped on a pair of navy blue driving gloves.

"Ready, Glenn?" Hersey had noticed his daughter leaning over the nearest window to the driveway. He stuck one gloved hand into the air as a gesture of good faith and spared no dramatics while lowering it towards the key that lay—idle for the past decade—in the ignition.

Hersey James's hand faded from its usual red into a pale cream color as he twisted the key to try for a start. Smirking, he held eye-contact with Glenn in the rearview mirror as he did it. The car sputtered and coughed a gray cloud of exhaust from the rear tail pipe. This relic of the seventies hadn't been meant for any kind of performance since the end of the Carter administration in 1981.

Hersey's proud smile faded further and further with each new attempt that he took at the ignition. His confidence had been replaced by a red heat that lit his face and shined in contrast to the stoicism of his navy blue attire.

"You okay down there?" Glenn called down from her perch on the window sill. She was being genuine, but her words came out with a kind of sarcasm that was otherwise foreign to her vocabulary. Hersey frowned up at her, only briefly, before climbing out the driver's side door and resigning himself back to the comforts of his own home. "You should have tried the other car!" Glenn said while her father slumped back up that same red marble staircase.

"Forget it." Hersey grumbled, he spoke towards his chest in defeat.

"C'mon, you were just having so much fun!" Glenn's persistent smile made a triumphant return to her lips.

"—You know, we could've really made a difference in the eighties." Hersey surprised his daughter with a sudden change of subject. His spine straightened and his beret seemed to fall further over his forehead.

"Who?"

"Us!" Hersey's voice adopted a husky kind of passion. "The show! The eighties *needed* a sense for adventure, a sense of exploration beyond what was right in front of their faces. They replaced *The James Gang* with what... *Alf*? Those producers plagued an entire decade when they canceled *my* show."

The room fell into Glenn's least favorite kind of silence, it was the kind that crept in because she was truly at a loss for words. Her father's face had turned beet red and bubbled as if his blood overinflated the flesh beneath his face. Glenn remained on the sill of the window, she had climbed over the coffee table and stuck her feet out so her Versace slippers hung off the other side of the sill. Slowly, they teetered away from the control of her toes.

Glenn's fingers fluttered around her torso, fidgeting around her hips and over the top of her silk nightgown in desperate search through the contents of her pockets. All of a sudden, she was *dying* for a cigarette. "The children of the eighties, *your* generation, they needed me." Suddenly, both Glenn and her father had matching cigarettes between their fingers. "Yes—Yes, they needed something in the real world. None of the escapist drivel that they were force-fed."

"Oh, come on Dad." Glenn's focus shifted out the window. Judging by her expression, you would think she was enthralled by something that stood far off in the distance. "Are the kids of my generation really that far gone? I mean, of course we were all raised by television, but I think that TV's been a pretty good parent to me. Don't I take good care of you? Haven't I turned into a well-adjusted and caring member of society?"

"Yes, my dear. Of course you have." The pride returned to Hersey's face. Even if he had been immobilized by the old age of both himself and his car collection, he always had Glenn to fall back on. One thing that was inarguably good, and he had put it into the world. "However, I do think that you're an exception. Think about it, you watched the same programs as your two older sisters and look how they turned out!" The red had drained from Hersey's face and his speech had adopted a great aura of nonchalance.

"Same programming..." Glenn began carefully, she drifted back into her polka-dotted seat as her attention turned back to the interior of the *James Gang* mansion. She sat down and softened her smile as if that were going to be enough to soften the blow of her coming words. "That calls for a steady diet of *James Gang* reruns."

Hersey gasped. His still-gloved hand raced to his chest and clutched at his heart while the rest of his body swayed as if an unfortunate gust of wind would've been enough to blow him away. For a moment, Hersey gave Glenn a sense that he had grown remarkably weak in his old age. She regretted her words as soon as they left her mouth.

After his moment of shock, Hersey James seemed to reset. His vulnerable moment of smallness had ceased and he brushed a wisp of white hair behind his ear as a way to illustrate a return to his long held illusion of strength.

"You always did have a way with words." Hersey's pride was returning against all odds, his eyes creased into crows feet as he smiled toward the light of his life. "And you've always been too good to those sisters of yours, they would never defend you like this."

With that last cutting remark from Hersey, almost as a period to the end of his sentence, a car's horn honked from the driveway. Glenn got up and approached the window once again, she talked as she glided across the room. She always *glided* when she walked.

"It's Henry Elliott! Won't you come down and say hi before we leave?"

"Not today." Hersey reached for a cigarette to tack onto the end of the one that was burning close to his lips by the time he gave up on it. "He makes me blue ever since we lost Will, and tonight is a night where I am already blue enough. You really shouldn't have brought your sisters up earlier."

"Kitty?"

"Who else?"

"Beatrice."

"Oh, yeah." Hersey placed his finger on his chin as if he had only just remembered his oldest daughter's existence. "Well, her too."

"What makes you say that?"

"You know how much I *despise* them." Hersey slumped towards his cigarette as opposed to the great effort that would have been required to lift it to his mouth.

"Since when?"

"What?"

"Beatrice and Kitty, since when have you *'despised'* them so much?"

"I don't know, maybe since my middle-daughter kidnapped Beatrice into her cult-like pact of hatred for her father! How about since the first time I picked up a tabloid after their twelfth birthdays! They have always resented me for not including them in *The James Gang*, I see no reason why I should not be allowed to hate them back." Hersey laughed in a husky tone, he laughed and the sound echoed back to Glenn another time around. Hersey laughed as if he was trying to shake the mansion from its foundation, he laughed as if he was trying to embarrass his daughters from across the globe.

"Fine then, if you're going to be like that you don't have to say hi. Even if he is the only son of your oldest and deadest friend. I'd better be going."

"Will wouldn't have wanted to speak with him either! Hey—Where are you going with him anyway?" Hersey yelled after his daughter, but he was too late. She had already glided out the door.

Henry's face was solemn when he met Glenn at the door, he scowled like he often had in his role as Henry James on *The James Gang*. The bad boy of the bunch, he was known for scowling directly into the camera during dramatic scenes in the show. "You ready?" He asked. His voice was huskier than usual, it was as if he'd been choking on something on his way to the mansion.

"Ready as I'll ever be."

With Glenn gone, Hersey took to wandering. He often did this when he found a moment alone. He liked to look at his things as if he were a straw-man, an imaginary stranger that was visiting the mansion for the first time. Someone who shared all of Hersey's deepest affinities for decor, eclectic furniture, memorabilia, literature, vinyl, feminist art, and the stylings of the 1970s.

Hersey ran his fingers along the nearest corner of his red oak grandfather clock. He imagined his hand as an admirer's touch, cautiously touching the artifact as the host of this fictional tour explained that this clock had arrived with the mansion's construction in the year 1900. Hersey passed from the foyer into his cavernous bedroom, he walked in imaginary awe at the building that he had lived in for the better part of three decades. Would they give tours after his death?

A stack of records sat at the foot of Hersey's king-sized Arabian bed, striped with patterns of royal purple and ivory stars that criss-crossed behind images of Cat Stevens and Paul McCartney. *Mona Bone Jakon*—Cat Stevens's album from 1970—was Hersey's current obsession.

He was meticulous as he slipped it out from its blue sleeve of protection. The sleeve had cracked and bent through decades of wear, but the interior remained immaculate. Careful as ever, Hersey placed the record onto the spindle and used his most expensive brush to swipe over the grooves three times to remove any dirt or dust that may have snuck its way onto the record to ruin its pristine sound. Only truly free when alone, Hersey kicked back onto his bed.

The needle traveled towards the edge of the record, hovering over the key to the music for a moment before lowering itself down to sweet connection with Hersey's most prized possession. His lips peeled into a smile that had an unmistakable resemblance to the one that Glenn flashed so often. "Lady D'Arbanville" had only just begun to open the album, and Hersey James had already shifted into a deep, sleeplike, state of grace. Cat Stevens's voice rang out from the speakers.

"My lady D'Arbanville, why do you sleep so—"
Ding Dong!
"And you will be my fill, yes, you will be my—"
Ding Dong!
However dreamlike Hersey's state of music-induced euphoria may have been, the second ringing of the front door's bell shook him wide awake. He halted the record with a huff of air that filtered out his nose and through the hairs in his mustache. One would have guessed that his breath reeked of cigarettes and coffee. If he ever let anyone get close enough to smell, that is.

Nothing could have redeemed the mortal sin that was interrupting Cat Stevens mid-song. Nothing, except the possibility that Glenn had come home early. Maybe she missed him? After all, what's a day out with friends when compared to time spent in the loving company of her family?

It didn't take long for Hersey to convince himself of the certainty of Glenn's return, so he raced back into the foyer and down the stairs. His smile had stretched into a full-on beam by the time he made it to the landing. There, he saw an elegant figure on the other side of the stained-glass windows. It must be Glenn, it swayed in the window that surrounded the mansion's heavy front door.

The figure's delicate silhouette appeared to be carrying something, but it all appeared as no more than a darker purple blob against a background of brighter purple glass.

Something silent pulled at the back of Hersey's brain. It tugged when he reached for the crystal doorknob that separated him from the light of his life, something silent told him to enjoy this alone time while he still had the chance... Obviously, this silent something had no clue how delightful Hersey found Glenn's company to be.

So, Hersey brushed his reservations to the side. He twisted the doorknob and pulled back on his last defense from the onslaught that could be the outside world. He opened the door: Enter Beatrice James.

Beatrice. Her dark green shoes matched a dark green pantsuit, a long fox-furred coat hung over the first layer of her outfit and swayed in the breeze of the world outside of the *James Gang* mansion. Her green knee bounced with impatient energy as if she had been keeping time. Her hip cocked to the right and met a hand. Three necklaces dangled, almost as delicate as her figure, down towards the space in between her breasts: One gold, one silver, and one green.

Beatrice's lips stretched and turned down towards her chin, they always turned down, just like they always came equipped with a cigarette to hang off from the corner of her mouth. A vaguely familiar face shifted its weight back and forth behind Beatrice. His cover seemed to be causing her a great deal of discomfort. Then again, discomfort had always been a sort of baseline emotion for the eldest daughter of the James family. The sight of Beatrice James sent a chill down the back of her father's spine. "Audrey Hepburn, in the flesh!" Hersey colored over his dread with excitement.

"You know I hate that comparison." Beatrice spoke a cloud of American Spirit brand smoke into her father's face. She applied a pair of bug-eyed sunglasses to cover up the massive eyes that tended to bring allusions to the movie star.

"Of course." Hersey smiled and stepped to the side to allow a pathway for his visitors to enter. The old man stepped up from behind her. He bowed at Hersey, shook his hand, and continued into the mansion as if he owned the place.

"We better hope he doesn't find your dungeon." Beatrice smirked as Hersey watched the old man disappearing into the basement. He limped when he walked.

"Who is that?" Hersey leaned towards his daughter, whispering his question while she leaned away from the mouth of cigarettes and coffee.

"Surely you're not that senile yet, are you?"

"I certainly hope not."

"That's a shame." Beatrice seemed to be doing her best Glenn James impression as she accepted her father's nonverbal welcome into the home. She glided and cocked her head towards the top floor of the mansion. She scanned over everything before her with a cold kind of evaluation in her eyes. "I had a dream last night where I inherited this place." She spun around on her heels and faced her father with a rare smile. "Of course, I kept *almost nothing* the way you have it right now."

"Oh?" Hersey asked, undaunted by this random attack on his skills in the field of interior decoration. "May I ask what remained?" He'd come to expect some stray shots over the years. "I mean, in such a detailed dream you must remember the *one* thing that remained the same from the home of your youth. Please, enlighten me."

"It's really not important."

"No, I insist." Hersey grew as his daughter shrank. She was suddenly so meek, a far cry from the brash woman that had glided into the room. Hersey could tell that Beatrice was embarrassed by her answer, and he found that all the more intriguing.

"Fine, if you're going to be so pushy about it. It was Glenn's room. Everything that you're responsible for; it was gone. But Glenn's room stayed exactly the same. I tried and tried to change it, but I couldn't." Hersey allowed himself to smile, this inkling of warmth was a new thing to come from the mouth of his most pessimistic daughter.

"I always knew she had the best eye in the house. Seems like all the distance between you two has offered some perspective!" Hersey beamed as he drifted from the doorway to join his daughter on the landing.

"She sees me around. Don't think I stopped existing when I started avoiding you." Beatrice lowered her cigarette into a blown-glass ashtray that had been sculpted into the shape of a blooming red rose. Her hands disappeared into the pockets of her coat, and she continued her speech. "I mean, somebody's got to keep this family together."

"Right, the family that I started." Hersey grumbled. "The family that excommunicated me without a second thought."

"Oh, come on Hersey." Beatrice pulled another cigarette out of the endless supply that hid in her coat-pocket. "You know Glenn would never allow for a *full* excommunication. I don't know what kind of spell you placed on that girl but she holds onto her attachment to you no matter what Kitty and I tell her." Beatrice took a long drag from her fresh American Spirit, soaking the conversational upper-hand in for as long as she could. "And don't act like you haven't earned our cold shoulder over the years."

To this, Hersey cleared his throat. He was at a loss for words. Then he cleared his throat again, and a third time. His time was filled with Glenn's company in those days, awkward silences like this one brought memories of the times when all three girls were living in the mansion together. Bad days. "You've spoken to Kitty?" Hersey forced the words out as if he were trying to give a speech while participating in New York's annual marathon. Beatrice rolled her eyes, no answer. "How's she doing?"

"Don't ask."

"No, really. I'd like to know."

"You know," Beatrice ditched her cigarette into the ashtray with about an inch left before it would've reached the filter. "You're so old now, I don't really see the point in sharing these kinds of problems with you anymore. Crisis management was never quite your strong suit, and now—"

"What? Now you think I'm gonna *die* before we have a chance to solve her? I may not be the picture of health, but I'm alive just like you! God knows I've kept you in the loop on days when you were *much* closer to the other side." Hersey gave Beatrice a side-eye. "She's an animal, don't you think I know that whether you tell me or not?"

The two oldest living Jameses stood—only about an arm's-length from each other—in another of the many milling silences that they had grown to expect over the course of their thirty-plus year entanglement into each other's lives. "You would've killed me yourself if you'd had the guts." Beatrice said "And besides—that's a real sore subject to bring up on the day of my return."

Beatrice refused the retention of any eye-contact with her father, and her gaze fell towards the floor to evoke memories from her days as a younger woman of the eighties. Her big mane had been tamed into a sleek side-part of black hair, and her glamorous makeup had been washed away until all that remained was a tasteful bit of coverup to hide the deepening of her new wrinkles. A lot had changed, Hersey thought, but her attitude only became more confident as the years passed by.

"Why did you come back here?" Hersey spoke with disdain that he hadn't meant to let on.

"Isn't my presence always welcome?"

"You avoid me, you just said it yourself. So what has made you come back here? Did you really convince yourself that I'd died last night? Were you coming by to check-in about your inheritance?" A smile peeked onto Hersey's lips, though it wasn't warm like the smiles that he had made a habit of sharing with Glenn. No, this one was competitive, almost vindictive.

"Let's sit down. Shouldn't I at least have some time to get comfortable before you start asking the tough questions? I should probably find Elroy anyway, he has a terrible habit of exploring *every* corner of a new place before making himself comfortable. I'll never understand senile old men—I'm sure you get it though." Beatrice spoke as she glided towards the stairs. "Wouldn't want him getting lost in a maze like this place!"

Hersey could have sworn that Beatrice was doing an impersonation of Glenn with her walk. She knew that would get under his skin. She knew how impressed he had always been with the way Glenn moved around the house. All the same, he followed her down the stairs and played it off as if he hadn't noticed a thing.

"Elroy!" Beatrice screeched when she reached the mansion's basement. The sound of her voice echoed throughout the dark, ballroom-like room that Hersey only dared to venture into when he was in the mood for a good fright.

Hersey's skin began to crawl when he heard the creaking patter of old footsteps that limped from a far off corner of the room. *"Elroy!"* Beatrice screeched with an increase of intensity.

"You really have turned quite motherly in your old age." Hersey teased. He meant to laugh at his own joke, but his basement-induced undercurrent of fear froze him to such a point that all he could manage was a cocky tilting of his wispy-haired head.

Beatrice opened her mouth for a third screech, but was interrupted by a rustling towards the far side of the room. Elroy had ceased his snail-paced dash towards the light right on the border of Hersey's field of vision. The basement faded into a deep kind of darkness, an underground kind of darkness, and Elroy waited at the edge of it. He spared no dramatics with his final step into complete visibility. It was slow, it was dignified.

Elroy stood with his arms folded behind his back. Gray hair peeled behind his ears and his tongue rested firmly against the inside of his cheek. "Hello, Hersey." Elroy smirked, he expected to be recognized and his head bobbed up and down in smug anticipation.

Hersey drifted over to Elroy, he extended a hand for their second shake in as many minutes. Hersey inspected the face that stood before him. "Elroy, I know that name, but the face has been swallowed by a much older man!" Hersey smiled.

"You're a fool if you think I'm not holding my tongue."
Elroy held his smirk steady.

"Are you still with *The Daily Dilemma*? I must admit
to my ignorance when it comes to the daily's of this era."

"Aren't you going to tell him why I'm here?" Elroy
turned back towards Beatrice, his capacity for play had all
but run out. He raised his voice, his tone hardened, and
his charisma drifted closer to annoyance. Beatrice rose to
a straight-backed position, and she spoke as if she had to
pry the words from her mouth.

"We've got an idea for you, Hersey." Beatrice spoke
too fast for Hersey's old ears to keep up. Her words blasted
out of a drooping mouth. They slurred together and hinted
at an undertone of sarcasm that never quite managed to
show through. All of this left Hersey in great perplexion,
so he looked to his old friend for answers.

"What is she talking about?" Hersey asked as Elroy
tipped further into anger towards Beatrice. The red-faced
man sealed his eyes tight, took three deep breaths, calmed
his face down to its regular shade of cream, and spoke with
a sense of grace that had been renewed.

"I haven't been paparazzi for a decade." Elroy exhaled
an impatient sigh. "I'm in show-business now. Some would
say that I stepped into the shoes that you left when you
disappeared from the world."

"So you came here to brag that you've cloned me?"
Hersey was losing his patience.

"I came to you because I need you!" Elroy placed a
hand on Hersey's shoulder, he flinched at the touch and
Elroy squeezed in response. "Think about this as your big
return to the limelight, the great renaissance of Hersey
James's career..." Elroy's eyes glazed over with a milky kind

of fog. "I'm picturing…" Elroy looked towards the ceiling of the basement as if it were his own personal telescope into heaven. *"James Gang: The Next Generation."*

"Oh, wow." A distant gleam came to Hersey's eye when he heard those hallowed words.

"You're still the star, I'll produce." Elroy started walking back on his former bravado. Slowly, Hersey lifted his gaze from Elroy's to Beatrice. She was squirming in place, leaning up against the wall. Still reluctant to meet her father's wandering eye with her own.

"That's why I brought him here. Don't say I never gave you anything." Beatrice scanned the marble floor that her father stood and fidgeted over.

"*I*—I don't know what to say." Hersey's mouth hung open as he searched for an answer to his own uncertainty. He seemed to be losing his balance as his attention bounced between Beatrice and Elroy like a pinball stuck between two bumpers in the machine. He landed back at Elroy in disbelief. "Thank you." A tear trembled and threatened to fall from the old man's eye. All this vulnerability aged him inside his cavern of a basement.

Hersey folded two shaky red hands in front of his hips. He rubbed his thumbs together, uncertain about whether or not it would be appropriate for him to hug this strange, conceited man of the past.

"Don't mention it." Elroy said. "It's Beatrice, actually. She's the one that convinced me of this being a good idea."

"Why would you do that?" Hersey's tone was only deepening with vulnerability. He turned his head back towards Beatrice and had to catch himself before the momentum of that tiny movement sent him tumbling backwards. Hersey's face had completed its turn to red. His eyebrows tilted up towards the brim of his blue beret, and his bottom lip stuck out with whiteness that pressed against his front teeth as they gritted with effort to remain composed. Beatrice's aura of discomfort evaporated in response, her cold stare hadn't blinked since her father stopped speaking.

"Don't think I did this to put a halo around my head." Beatrice loomed large with intimidation as she pried herself away from the comfort of her spot on the wall. "Your big break's only coming with Elroy's help, and that help leaves if I leave—"

"What do you want?" Hersey struggled to harden himself. Both Beatrice and Elroy's smiles tinged with avarice, though the basement's harsh lighting was doing no favors for the duo of ultra-fair-complected social climbers.

"I want a part." Beatrice tilted her nose up towards the light that interrogated above her head. She locked in on her father's face, studying each twitch and quiver that rippled across his cheek before deciding that the drama of the moment had reached its peak. "Glenn's part."

Hersey James hadn't been described as *childlike* one day in his entire life. He tended to operate with the kind of high head that conjured speculation about whether or not he had *ever* been a child. His company had always been much younger than he, and his monochromed outfit and feathering hair gave him an air of blankness when it came to outside speculation about his age.

The Don of the James family, the removed one, the old man that had always loomed so large and so esoteric above every one of the family's operations, shrunk to a whisper in the basement that afternoon. "*Beatrice*—I don't think I can do that to Glenn." Hersey's voice grew hoarse, an echo of the scream that refused to be heard.

"Why not?" Beatrice started to speak by squaring her shoulders to the father that wilted before her. "You did it to me and Kitty the first time around and that didn't seem to bother you very much!"

"That was different." Hersey declared. He spoke with authority that echoed in a rumble that rattled the tinny walls of the mansion's basement.

"Right. How dare I expect you to share your ugly side with the world?" Beatrice's ire was fading into the pale blue of melancholy. She could've predicted the path of this conversation from miles away. Hersey paused for a moment, he had achieved an aloofness in his stare and his hands traveled deep into the pockets of his navy blue slacks, he drifted back towards the stairs that they had only just come down.

"You know, you always were my most difficult daughter."

"I bet you liked my fictional counterpart a whole bunch though. What was her name again?" Beatrice shuffled her feet as she spoke, drifting upstairs with her father, confused by his gradual exit but not ready for this conversation to end. Not willing to allow for silence until that name had been etched into the soft ooze of her mind.

"It was Gretchen, Gretchen Williams."

"I'll bet it hurt to watch while your own father replaced you on national TV." Elroy drifted back into the conversation. He spoke in a dazed kind of whisper, like he hadn't meant to speak aloud.

"It did!" Beatrice strained to mask her excitement in answering that question, but the realization of a crowd for this debate was too exhilarating to hide. "He let them use their real first names and everything! *'Gretchen James'*, she really was everything you wanted me to be. Wasn't she, dad?" Beatrice *never* called her father *'dad'*, he had been nothing more than a Hersey to her for as long as she could remember. "All the better for pretending that she's your real daughter, all the better for pretending that Beatrice doesn't exist." Beatrice's shuffle had cornered her father into the stairwell and backed him up the stairs to the foyer.

"Surely this can't be how you conduct all your business dealings!" Hersey projected his words although his daughter was only a few feet away. He spoke from the depths of his chest with a bass that washed the room clean of all other noise. The echoes came back in silence. "Come into my office." Hersey cracked a squinty-eyed smile that covered his face in the steps of crow's feet.

Beatrice blushed as she mosied into another polka-dotted chair. Her face heated from cream to a rose, perhaps she had come on too strong with the blame. Elroy was quiet when he took a seat, criss-crossed in a chair next to Beatrice as they faced the desk that towered over them from the other side of the room. Gone was the former reporter with the big ideas and the Hollywood address, the meek old man had faded into silence.

Hersey's desk was a dark, heavy, beast of furniture. It was the same teak table that had once been used as a station to sign thousands of fan-mail signatures in the days of the original *James Gang*. It had been carved by none other than Hersey's long-lost best-friend and director, William Elliott. Scenes of sailing boats and jumping fish lined the edges of the desk and gave Hersey a groove to run his ever-fidgeting fingers through as he sat down. William Elliott always had a thing for the sea.

"So…" Hersey reached a hand down to the side of his throne and emerged with three cigarettes. He extended one to Beatrice and flinched towards Elroy before dropping the second and placing the third one in his own mouth. "You've come here to blackmail me?" Hersey spoke in a dignified manner, whatever softening that happened in the basement had calloused back over again. Hersey was back, his stare towards Beatrice was heavy.

"I don't know if I'd say that." Elroy smiled with eyes that seemed like they were trying to pull Hersey down from his throne. The old man's eyes were blue with flecks of silver and black that warred for dominance over such a vibrant area of the otherwise barren face. "Words like *'blackmail'* seem a bit harsh, don't they?" Drops of rain began to *tick* off the windows that lined the wall behind Hersey, the *ticking* noise turned into large *plops* as the weather outside snapped into a total downpour. "Remember Mexico?" Elroy began to smile. "We have too much history to boil this down to something as simple as—"

"Don't patronize him."

Hersey frowned towards Elroy before realizing that his daughter had come to his defense. Angry pride turned into confusion and Hersey tilted his head towards Beatrice, beckoning her into elaboration. "Hersey's an old man, Elroy. Maybe even older than you." Beatrice turned towards the seat to her left. "Don't do that to him. He may be crazy, but he's wise enough to know what we're doing here. A bit of honesty's the least we could do."

Beatrice flipped her shining black hair over towards Hersey before ending her statement with a long drag from the cigarette that her father had gifted her. It was the most common generosity that *The James Gang* knew. Beatrice parted her crested lips to form a circle with her mouth, and just as she began to embark on the drawn out journey of an exhale, the doorbell rang from the foyer behind her.

Elroy and Hersey flinched in near-unison when they heard that sound, their eyes snapped towards the door with what was either excitement or anxiety. Beatrice, however, was unphased. She regained the attention of the other two by lowering her voice to the tone of a deep chant. Her sound resembled her sister Kitty's with such levels of feminine bass. "We know *exactly* what we're doing." Beatrice zeroed in on Hersey's eyes. She placed her sunglasses in the lap of her forest green pantsuit, and allowed her eyes to bulge towards her father with great intensity. "Now, I'll get the door. But we're *far* from done here."

The fox-furred coat flapped over Hersey's desk as Beatrice turned and exited the room. Beatrice *clomped* away and Hersey found himself alone in the office with Elroy. The sound of the rain on the windows integrated with the *clomping* sound of Beatrice's fading high-heels. The two old men were left with no noise to cover the space between them. "Excuse me, Elroy?" Hersey crossed his legs and leaned over the desk to see the man that sat so low beneath him. "Would you mind explaining something for me?"

"Oh—" Elroy started, perplexed, as if he expected complete silence between the two of them in Beatrice's absence. "I don't know how professional it is to discuss this any further until Beatrice comes back." Elroy smiled a politician's smile, one that refused to show his teeth. The smile faded when he looked down, and his attitude took a sudden left turn. "You know, I owe a lot of my success to the access you gave me back then. I don't think I ever got the chance to thank you." Silence ensued apart from the rain's *tick*, Elroy's eyelids shuttered before he spoke again. "And you never blamed me for what happened. You could have ruined my career after that, but you didn't..."

"Should I have?" Hersey blurted his question. He looked as if he were going to yell for a minute, but he caught himself before losing control. "You're welcome, those were the best days of my life and I'm far too old to blame a man for his honesty." Hersey paused and smiled, nodding his head politely. "You loved Glenn back then. That's the mark of a good man in my book." Hersey paused again to sigh. "About my question; surely it won't change my reaction to your proposition. It really is just a curiosity of mine."

"You can ask, but in no way does that guarantee an answer." Elroy's smile returned as he spoke. Only now, Hersey had joined him with a more enthusiastic kind of grin.

"Okay." Hersey leaned back in his chair and twirled his thumbs as if he were deep in thought. "I just have one question, then I'll leave you alone. All I have is one thing to say and then we can sit in perfect silence until my daughter comes back." Hersey leaned forward again to make sure that Elroy was well aware of the words he was saying. "I suppose Beatrice wants a part because she thinks it'll turn her into some kind of darling of the audience. Maybe some kind of darling to me, too."

"I suppose she could." Elroy answered in a voice that was strained. "That's not a question though."

"I'll get to that." Hersey assured the old man with a wave of his hand. "And I suppose she is smart enough to recognize the fact that each child in the show has always acted as a shade of their real life counterpart's personality."

"I suppose she is."

"Then wouldn't it be easier for her to update Gretchen's role? I mean, she'd be acting as herself that way. Why must she take the role from her own sister?"

Elroy shifted his weight to the other side of his seat, he sculpted his hair behind his ears and he sucked on the office's air with a *hiss*. "Sisters." He smiled. "There's always something to prove."

Beatrice stared into the stained glass window while her hand hovered over her father's front door crystal knob. She had always despised Hersey for his flamboyance when it came to exhibitions of their wealth. She found embarrassment in the priceless paintings, high-ceilings, and museum-esque quality of the mansion that she had grown up in. She had always blamed her father for designating her to a life that had been infected by the abstraction of guilt that she found in her own intense materialism.

Now, hovering her hand so close to the crystal doorknob, the de facto *'welcome'* sign for the screaming kind of elegance that Beatrice had grown to despise so much, she drew her hand back.

Beatrice took a moment to study the shadowy silhouette that shined through from the other side of the entrance. All of a sudden, Beatrice felt a great deal of pity for the naivete of this figure. She wanted to scream through the glass, to tell it to turn and run before the mansion sucked it in with the charm of its old-fashioned elegance. Before Hersey had a chance to sink his claws in to drain it of all its life. Before everything it once valued had been replaced by an elegant object or an article of clothing.

Beatrice's focus shifted away from the shadow of the figure on the other side of the door. The depth of her vision shortened and she found herself staring at her own solemn face in the window's reflection. "No more James's." She said out loud.

The doorbell rang again, this time it carried a tone of exasperation as if it knew that somebody was stalling on their way to answering it. This second ring managed to bring Beatrice back to reality. She looked at her hand to find that it had clenched onto the crystal doorknob. In the midst of her introspection, Beatrice had clamped her hand onto the crystal so hard that a sharper edge might have sliced her palm all the way to the bone.

Beatrice was keenly aware of the blood that pooled from the small cut that had formed on her palm, the crystal doorknob was cool against the heat of her wound. She looked at the pitiful figure that mirrored her from the other side of the window. She despised it for its patience, she despised it for wanting to enter. Blood ran down Beatrice's fingertips, it oozed with connectedness and felt as if she were staking a claim by allowing it to fall into the depths of the carpeted entryway. It was this exact moment of pitiful scorn that tempted Beatrice into opening the door.

Glenn James stood on the other side of the entryway. Her cheeks were red and shiny, her blonde hair had wetted into something more solid that she pulled behind her ears. Glenn couldn't help herself from looking remarkably young when facing her older sister, she had not been lined in such an intricate kind of roadmap like her sister had. No folds or creases came from the smile that stretched across Glenn's face. She delighted at the sight of this new company.

"Beatrice James, back where she belongs!" Glenn wrapped her older sister into an over-enthusiastic embrace and pronounced all of her *'Bs'* with the spitting stammer of a *Looney Tune*. Both girls ejected from their brief hug with buggy realization in their eyes, though that had never been a hard thing to evoke for Beatrice *'Audrey Hepburn'* James. "You're bleeding!" Glenn shouted in a hoarsely raised voice.

"You're crying!" Beatrice took a step towards her sister for a better look at the tears. The cheek-to-cheek embrace had clued Beatrice into a certain kind of salt that came from Glenn's cheek. Not all that was wet had been caused by the rain.

"Come on." Glenn turned her shoulders back towards the driveway, coaxing Beatrice away from the mansion. "Let's protect that cut before you go and dye the whole carpet red. I have a bandage in the car." She glanced at the red splotch that Beatrice's cut had left on the cream-colored carpet. Its splatter had separated and fallen in a curious kind of shape that looked like five fingers on a hand. Five fingers that spread out and menaced, even in their form as a benign print on the carpet. Beatrice studied the mark for a moment before following her sister out to the driveway.

"You look healthy. Other than the blood, I mean." Glenn opened the door to the car that was parked at the end of the driveway, blocking Hersey's relics in while it enjoyed the majority of the front yard's room for itself. Beatrice climbed in after Glenn, the stately Jeep was too big to be practical for either of the girls. Glenn reached into her glove box and came out with a cotton pad in one hand and a brown glass bottle of isopropyl alcohol in the other.

"Is it healthy, or am I just less strung out?" Beatrice spoke in a tone that was needlessly hushed. Just about every literate American had heard of Beatrice James's infamous entanglements to the world of pills and powders.

It was big news, and it had teetered in and out of the headlines for the better part of the past two decades. Still, she felt the need to turn the topic into a whispering matter.

"Both, I guess." Glenn rustled through the clutter in her glove box, looking for a band aid among the surprising mess that resided in the car of the neatest member of *The James Gang.* "I mean, you were pretty far gone when I saw you at Henry's party on New Year's Eve."

"Hm." Beatrice squirmed while applying alcoholic pressure on one hand with the other. "I suppose it's not so hard to beat the way I looked that night, is it?" Both girls smiled in half measures before turning their attention away from each other: Beatrice, focusing on the pulsations of her cut, and Glenn, whose attention had been stolen by the details on her intricately painted fingernails.

"I don't know why I mentioned his name." Glenn's eye sank deeper into the study on the tips of her fingers. "I'm sorry." To this, Beatrice offered no response. She winced at the sensation of the alcohol dripping into her hand. The foreign substance provided a depth of feeling that had proven impossible for her to produce inwardly, no matter how hard she tried. The pad numbed her hand and alleviated it of any and all feeling, it was narcotic and sour and intruding into her flesh. Even as she released the pad and spread a bandaid over the top of the cut, the sensation remained bubbling beneath her skin.

Beatrice had turned into such a slave to this feeling by the time Glenn spoke that her words all but ceased to resonate among the distractions in her mind. Each word that Glenn spoke was like a single raindrop that amounted to no more than a small speck among the deeper depth of her profound numbness. Still, one word managed to seep through her wall of immunity, one word that pushed her back from that more general sense of stinging bliss. Henry.

Henry James on the show, Henry Elliott in real life. The host of this particular New Year's Eve bash had made a name for himself as the second oldest child of Hersey James on the original *James Gang* TV show. Dressed in brown overalls and accompanying this look with various colors of stocking caps and work boots, he was a carbon copy of his real-life counterpart, Kitty James.

It had been a surprise when the girls received their first invite to Henry's annual party about five years ago. Each sister had their own sordid history with the former star, and Kitty couldn't even bear to look at the boy for longer than two blinks without choking on her own spit. Still, they went, and the threesome returned every year like clockwork.

It wasn't a particularly good party, Henry's penthouse was drafty and uninteresting to a James's naturally decorative eye. They went because Glenn had always kept a foot in both circles, the real and the television versions of *The James Gang*, that is. For Beatrice and Kitty, however, to decline this invitation was to admit defeat, an admittance of truth to the perception that they were members of the inferior society. The version of *The James Gang* that wasn't fit for TV, the version of *The James Gang* that deserved to be hidden from the world.

"It's okay." Beatrice spoke, even though the invocation of Henry's name caused her a great deal of discomfort. "I'm not Kitty."

"Right, and I won't say her name either. *Er*— Gretchen, not Kitty."

"You did it anyway, didn't you?" Beatrice smiled, and her sister planted a scolding hand over her own mouth. "You shouldn't worry." Beatrice laughed to herself. "I'm not quite so frail these days. I actually made Hersey remind me of her name earlier just so he had to acknowledge it!" Glenn refused to join Beatrice in her laughter. Instead, pulling a cigarette from her lavender handbag, she scrunched her eyebrows towards the center of her forehead and hinted at a sense of concern.

"Is that why you came back then, to antagonize our father?" Glenn crossed her delicate legs and pulled on the cigarette's filter with her lips.

"You smoke in your car?" Beatrice's smile faded and Glenn turned the key to ignite its engine.

"Of course I do." Glenn said. "Let's get out of here. Want to go to Lamont's for lunch?"

"Aren't you going to offer one to me?" Beatrice held a bloody hand towards Glenn's cigarette in expectation of an offering.

"Aren't you going to tell me why you've returned?" Glenn's eyes narrowed. Her lips released the cigarette, but her hand kept resting limply near her face. The other hand twisted against the steering wheel and she locked the car's doors.

"Let's go to lunch." Beatrice smiled with a glance that darted to the window where Hersey sat across from Elroy.

The two girls drove off, summer colors lined the roads with green that made Beatrice think of Kitty. She lived for days like this. Beatrice's thoughts of Kitty were brief, there hadn't been much recent news to stoke the imagination lately. It was as if she had ceased to exist.

Instead, Beatrice envisioned the scene back at the mansion. Elroy duking it out with Hersey over the future of *James Gang: The Next Generation*. She couldn't help herself, she snickered out loud when she imagined the embarrassment of her father's defeat. Hersey had been good in his day, no doubt. But Elroy had no match once he got started with a debate.

"What's so funny?" Glenn asked, keeping her eyes on the road and smiling her good natured smile. It pained Beatrice to hurt Glenn like this, but it was no more than a speck of pain compared to the torture that Beatrice had to experience over the years. She shrugged.

"Nothing." Beatrice smiled. "I'm just glad to get some time alone with you, I feel like it's been *ages*." Glenn pulled the car into a reserved spot within the extensive parking lot that surrounded Lamont's Bistro.

Glenn ordered a beet salad and a vodka soda, she giggled every time the waitress walked by and she called everybody by their first name. Beatrice ordered a steak, well done. Whatever took the longest to cook, whatever kept Glenn away from the mansion. "Well done? You won't taste a thing!" Glenn protested Beatrice's order in a voice that promised not to cause a scene.

"I know what I like." Beatrice stuck her nose into the air and Glenn sighed as if she were about to admit to something that carried real weight. "What's wrong?" Beatrice noticed the look on her face.

"Nothing." Glenn smiled like she did when she was on camera. "You really should reconsider that order of yours. What would Kitty say about all that meat? You're cooking it so much that it'll taste like tofu anyway." Glenn sighed again, and Beatrice furrowed her brow.

"Kitty's not here." That same brow raised, and Beatrice focused on her glass of water. "Have you heard anything out of her lately?"

"Radio silence." Glenn sighed her subtlest sigh of the past ten minutes. "*I mean*—I don't expect a letter every weekend, but days pass when I can't even remember the sound of her voice!" Glenn sighed again, without any subtlety this time.

"You're not actually upset about that, though. Are you?" Beatrice knew the answer to her question. Still, Glenn tried to defend herself.

"Of course I am. My own sister's a stranger!"

"No." Beatrice exclaimed. "You were crying when I opened the door for you, and now you're sighing up a storm like somethings *really* bothering you! You are Glenn James who never cries unless it's for the beauty of a bird, where were you?" Beatrice leaned down and dipped her chest onto the table, she asked her questions with wide eyes. Eager to incriminate.

Just then, Glenn broke into tears. The waitress slid the salad under her nose and she got tears all over her beets.

The restaurant was a dark one, even during lunch time. It was always filled; wall to wall with men in tuxedos and women that could only have been on their way to the prom. It just so happens that these are two archetypes of people that are particularly discomforted by the sound of crying.

Glenn's cry started out as a dribble of tears running away from the corners of her eyes, she was wailing by the time Beatrice got her steak.

"Glenn?" Beatrice asked. "Glenn, won't you tell me what's wrong? You can tell me." Beatrice spoke softly, as if her voice's quiet would counteract Glenn's loud. "Glenn? You know you can tell me, Glenn?" Beatrice repeated, this time with a piece of steak mashing inside of her mouth. Finally, Glenn sputtered in response.

Beatrice looked like a ghost when she floated back into the office of the *James Gang* mansion about an hour later.

Her entire face quivered and she wobbled with weak knees while she walked. "My God, we thought you'd been kidnapped! Who was at the door? Where have you been?" Hersey yelled. "It sounded like Glenn. I hope you didn't rat yourself out about this little scheme you're cooking up."

"It was Glenn." Beatrice bit at the end of her sentence, it was as if she were trying to swallow her words as they came out. "She said she wants to be alone, she won't be bothering us."

"Thank God, this really is a dirty trick you're trying to pull."

"And you're right here with me. Aren't you?" Beatrice spoke as she scanned the edge of Hersey's desk with avarice eyes. She watched as Hersey thumbed the engraving of a pink salmon over and over again, she watched while sweat dripped from his palm through his fingertips, she watched while he squirmed in the throne that had once seemed so remarkably comfortable.

Hersey crossed his legs for a matter of seconds. One second, really. Then he uncrossed them and leaned onto his elbows. He menaced over the teak desk with an accusatory finger extended in Beatrice's direction. He furrowed his brow to match his furrowed mustache, his finger twitched and trembled as it aimed for his daughter. "*You* were the one who showed up here unannounced, *you* were the one who brought Glenn into this mess, *you* are the one trying to steal the role that your sister earned when she was a child! Don't ever question my loyalty when it comes to my daughter! I'm *not* here with you, I am a captive in my own home."

Bug-eyed, Beatrice batted her lashes at the father that scolded her. She scanned the profile before her, she enjoyed the power that she had displayed by getting such a reaction out of the man. Beatrice held her father's gaze like a delicate vase as she stood up. She placed both of her hands along the edge of Hersey's desk. She ran her right hand along the engraving of a wave that crashed into the bow of a sailboat.

"Where was that loyalty the first time around?"

Hersey's furrowed brow began to glare at his daughter. The rain slowed behind him as he sucked on his teeth and narrowed his bloodshot eyes into a face that alluded towards thought. "I know you want this show." Beatrice continued. "I know this is the second chance that you've always wanted. I'm willing to give that to you if you meet me halfway." The air in the office had gone stale around their discussion. The rain was slowing and the only *tick* that was left to be heard in the background came from the red clock that kept time in a faint tone above Elroy's head.

Hersey leaned forward, he even thought about holding his daughter's hand, and he spoke with a newfound gentleness in his tone. "Beatrice, darling. Why can't you just take Gretchen's role? You'd be playing to your real personality and everyone could be happy."

Beatrice's eyes narrowed at the sound of Hersey's question. "Because you've got thick skin, Hersey." She smiled though it pained her to move her cheeks. "Because Glenn isn't one of us until she's been betrayed by you. Respectfully."

"*Respectfully?* What, am I supposed to neglect my other daughter for *your* benefit?" Hersey leaned down towards Beatrice, his stance bordered on being one of violence. His voice was strong with reckless venom, this tone was raspy and he was short of breath. "You've ridiculed this show for your entire life. You've skipped out on your family and disappointed your father at every turn. You're no Glenn, you'll never—"

"—Do you want this show to happen or not?" Beatrice stood up straight, there was a sense of finality to the gesture of her interjection. With a straight back and a rising smile, Beatrice sat like a snobbish statue of liberty in her green outfit. Hersey stared into the unflinching eyes that his daughter met him with. The bloodshot ones beaded over while the Hepburn ones narrowed in their obstinance. Slowly, and with an audible sigh that filled his mustache with smoke, Hersey James bowed his head.

"Of course I want the show." Hersey stared through stinging eyes that trembled and narrowed into a scowl. It pained him, admitting his own lust. Once again, the sound of the bell rang out from the front door of the *James Gang* mansion.

Beatrice and Elroy followed Hersey down the stairs like blood circling in a drain. Hersey's boat shoes clapped against the red marble staircase and contrasted the color of the floor like an American flag of interior decoration. The old man's face had clenched into such a tight fist of frustration that his eyebrow and mustache melted into one facial-bush that pushed towards and almost entirely covered his nose.

Glenn had come home with Beatrice, only she didn't make it past the foyer's bathroom before collapsing over the sink in another fit of tears. She emerged with the sound of the bell.

Glenn failed to offer any of her sister's theatrics while answering the door. There was no deep inspection through the window this time, no deep reflection into her own reflection against the stained glass, nor the crystal doorknob, nor her father's tendency towards flamboyance. No blood was to be spilled for this answering of the door. Just a sniffling smile and a twist of the doorknob. It all came so simply for the girl with the tears on her gown.

The heavy door pulled open. It creaked with dog-whistle-like pitch and screeched the entryway into a deeper depth of both silence and attention. It exposed the room to the sound of the rain that had picked back up with frequent spells of thunder and lightning outside. There, Kitty James stood, disturbed and pale to the point of appearing gray, in the doorway.

❧1979❧

Camera clicks mixed in with bird sounds in the front yard of the *James Gang* mansion. Hersey James donned a pair of Ray-Ban sunglasses before leaving for the day, camera flash had melted his pupils and burned the whites of his eyes into reds over the years. Two sparrows chirped overhead, but a camera's flash screamed and they evacuated the scene. "Hersey, Hersey James! How does it feel to know that your daughter has been spotted in Mexico?" Hersey flicked his sunglasses down from his nose and squared his shoulders at the reporter.

"Which daughter?" He asked.

"Beatrice, of course." The reporter jammed his camera into an angle that looked up at Hersey and equated him to a giant in the view of the lens. "Are you going to send her to rehab again? Is that where you're heading off to know? What makes you so confident about her recovery this time around? Who are you wearing?" The reporter flicked at the shutter of his camera, inching himself backwards as Hersey began to lower himself into the driver's seat of his 1975 Jaguar XJS.

"Elroy." Hersey shielded his mouth with his hand, addressing the reporter by name. "You know I don't have a comment for you." He smirked and flicked his sunglasses back over the bridge of his nose. "And won't you please back up? Glenn's on her way out and I don't want that camera of yours to blind her before her sixth birthday." Hersey slammed the car's cream colored door, waited a moment, and cranked the window down to open himself back up to the public. Another reporter ventured around the side of the *James Gang* mansion.

"He's over here!" Elroy said. He waved his hand good-naturedly and pointed through the open window of Hersey's car. One camera appeared, then another, then four more, a storm of camera toting Elroy lookalikes trudged out from around the side of the house.

"Can you tell me more about the state of Beatrice's health?"

"What's coming up for *The James Gang*?"

"Do you blame yourself for what's happening to your daughters?" The questions peppered into the car like a smoothie of mixed up words that stood on top of each other and scrambled into an ignorable level of incoherence. Hersey flashed a winning smile at the crowd before cranking his window back shut.

Just as Hersey shut himself off, the mansion's front door creaked to snag the attention of the crowding press. Little Glenn James popped her head out from the crack she made, famous blonde hair cascaded down her back in a ponytail and she frowned at the parade of grown men that clammored towards her from the car. Glenn faced a similar barrage of Beatrice-themed questions, the only difference being an occasional "What's your favorite color?" or "How are the ABC's coming along?" They watered themselves down for the sake of their own fading moral compasses.

Each media member referred to Glenn on a first name basis, and they all smiled when they noticed her's. Glenn James—queen of her media training class since before potty training—kept her head high and her mouth shut while she bopped through the crowd. She gave nothing but an agreeable smile to the cameras until she reached the back door of the car.

"C'mon Glenn, we haven't got all day!" Hersey yelled from his post in the driver's seat, but Glenn turned her back to the car door and allowed each reporter to catch up. They gathered around her and waited in a collective hush for the five year-old to hold court.

Glenn closed her eyes for a deep, meditative breath. She opened back up in conjunction with one word. "Shame!" Her smile flipped over and her eyebrows grew strong as she prepared to scold. "You should all be ashamed of yourselves! My sister is struggling, and we James's are going to do everything in our power to make sure that she's okay. That being said, this is a matter that we would like to handle in private. That's what's best for Beatrice, and we would appreciate it if you would respect that too." Glenn let the smile back onto her lips and she folded her hands into a stack at her lap. "And if you must know, I can do the ABC's backwards."

Rapid-firing camera clicks provided a soundtrack for Glenn as she turned her back to the reporters and climbed into her car seat behind Hersey.

"You should ignore them." Hersey grumbled as Glenn buckled up. "Reporters are a tool; give them as little as possible and you'll be able to live with them forever. Meet them on their terms, and you're sure to end up like your sisters before too long." The car started and Hersey began to back out of the driveway before the coast had cleared of reporters. Elroy was last in the scramble out from the car's path, and a reversing tire pressed down on the edge of his little toe as he tried to escape. His shriek—a bone-chilling 'aargh' sound—brought the entirety of the New York paparazzi to his aid. Hersey stuck a middle-finger out of his window as he drove away.

"You call that ignoring them?" Glenn piped up, turning around in her seat to examine her father's crime scene as she spoke. "I call that assault." Glenn's high-pitched voice took longer than usual to clear its sound from the air. Hersey clicked his tongue halfway through the process of opening his mouth in self-defense. Glenn chimed back in. "Are we going to see her?" Hersey growled in silence as his daughter spoke.

"Nobody likes an interrupter, now." Hersey pasted a fatherly tone over his annoyance. "It's not assault because we were defending ourselves against the intruders, okay? Nobody can hurt you in the *James Gang* mansion. And if they do, you have every right to assert yourself like I just did."

"Are we going to see her, Dad?" Glenn made sure to wait until well after Hersey finished speaking to talk this time. "I mean, just to make sure she's okay?"

"No." Hersey said. "We have a job to do and we can't make an exception to our work just because your sister decided that she wants to go hunting for headlines this week." Hersey sped up so abruptly that Glenn grabbed onto the door handle to brace herself. "You wouldn't want to disappear from the rest of *The James Gang*, would you?"

"I would never—"

"Good! Then it's decided." Hersey smiled into the rearview mirror. Letting out some air, he let off of the gas pedal at the same time.

The sun was bright over the boroughs that day, the set was bustling with people that fanned themselves and yanked at their T-shirts while they worked. Crowds of workers gathered to cool in what little shade the set's lot provided, and Hersey groaned as he parked and opened his door to the heat that had intensified since he left the mansion. "My God, this is terrible." He dabbed at his own bushy eyebrows with the cuff of the blue raincoat that never came off. Trying to stop the sweat from touching his ever-irritated eyes, Hersey squinted at Glenn as he watched her rise to her feet. "Well, whaddya think?" He asked.

"What do you mean?" Glenn squinted with confusion as Hersey did with pain.

"Would Beatrice go to Mexico for you if you were in her position? Or would she stay and fight for the people that *really* care about her?" Hersey gestured an arm out towards the set's entrance like a magic wand. "You can play this game from your high horse like you always do—go to Mexico and see what happens if you'd like—just don't expect the world, or the show, to stop for you while you're gone."

The two James's began trudging towards the set, the heat turned each step into something sticky that made Glenn wonder if her shoes might be melting. She looked down to study the heat of the final steps while her father shook hands with just about everyone he laid eyes on. *The James Gang* had arrived.

"Welcome Mr. James!"

"William! Tell me, my friend. Where will our adventures take us today?" Hersey's face lit up when he saw the white-haired man that sat to the left of the set's entrance.

William Elliott had been the director of the *The James Gang* since its second season, his direction has often been credited as the X-factor that turned the show into the behemoth of family adventure programming that it became in the winter of 1972. His direction—though intensely meticulous and demanding of his actors—combined with his role as father of the world-famous Henry Elliott, to turn the production of *The James Gang* into a real family business in the eyes of the press. A narrative that only deepened when Glenn joined her father on the cast in November 1978.

William stood up just in time for Hersey to wrap him into a playful headlock, they walked and talked and Glenn dragged further behind her father. "Haven't you seen?" William said, his voice carried a hint of trepidation that loosened Hersey's grasp. Hersey slowed his walk and strained his neck in an attempt to look around the corner to the stage where his beloved live audience was waiting for him. He bit at the air, unable to move but towards the pull of their adoration.

"Seen what?" Hersey measured his words and William got red in the face. William stopped the walk that Hersey had been slowing, he placed one hand on either side of Hersey's shoulders and took on a sobering tone.

"Maybe we should skip the recording today." William said while Glenn made a quiet return to the group.

"What?" Hersey recoiled. "You've gotta be kidding me, William. Eight whole seasons and we've *never* missed a show!"

"I know." William bowed his head in distress. "*Ma—* Maybe you should see this for yourself." Placing one hand on Hersey's back, William steered the patriarch of *The James Gang* towards the stage.

Hersey James pulled at the edge of his trademark beret, and William guided him to the edge of the stage where the audience was sure to recognize him. He braced for an inevitable blasting of cheers—even a walk down the street or a trip to Loomis's Spirits had a tendency to end that way in these days—Hersey took an extra step towards the middle of the stage, no applause.

Hersey released his grip on the edge of his beret, he unveiled his face to the live studio audience with a showy smile that glinted beneath the stage lights. Still, no applause. The show's usual audience would generally have consisted of raucous children and parents that came with the energy of a college football team and treated Hersey as if he were the fifth Beatle or the second coming of Jesus Christ. This time, Hersey looked out to a sea of disapproving faces; crossed legs, shaking heads, and all.

The energy was soon to come, all that it takes is a single outspoken soul to set a tone for the rest of the crowd to pile onto, and Hersey shuttered when the familiar swelling took its course. *Boos* cascaded from the spectating seats to the stage, Hersey shielded his face with his hands and recoiled from the blast. He glared at William, who waited just off to the side of the stage with a face that had turned green in reaction to the *booing*. "What's going on?" Hersey mouthed his words with wild eyes, still covering his face from the audience.

Just then, a stageside group of three particularly rowdy teenagers stood up. One held a sign, one adjusted her glasses, and the third bit at both sides of her cheeks. "America's father figure: Liar, coward, deadbeat!" The first girl's sign read.

"Where's Beatrice?" The second girl shrieked while the third hocked an impressive loogie that landed on the laces of Hersey's right boat shoe.

"Hey!" Hersey uncovered his face with a whip of his arm. "Show some respect!" He spat when he yelled. The audience consisted of people that appeared remarkably close to Beatrice's age, this wasn't the regular crowd. Finally, William shuffled onto stage, he tugged at Hersey's sleeve and hid his own face from the audience. He leaned in and covered them both as he muttered diffusing things into Hersey's ear. He hissed an impressive stream of extinguishing speech, but Hersey pulled away from his grasp.

"Be-a-trice! Be-a-trice! Be-a-trice! Be-a-trice!" The crowd broke into a chant and Hersey shook his head at its lack of creativity before stepping to the front of the stage.

"Hersey!" William whispered in a tone so shrill that it pierced through the sound of the crowd to grab Hersey's attention. William stepped up and twisted Hersey's shoulders towards the back of the stage. "Look!"

Wooden white beaches and plastic palm trees that grew on the edge of the stagnant water. *"The James Gang... In Mexico!"* The words hung from a sign near the top of the stage. Heavy light poured in from brighter, warmer lights than usual, and the beach's wooden background gave gradual way to a layer of actual sand that covered the ground. "Holy terrible timing." Hersey whispered to himself, gawking with wide-eyes that stuck on the sign that swayed above his head.

"It's a disgusting coincidence. But that's all it is. I swear that's all it is." William whispered. Still grasping Hersey by the shoulders, he started to shift his pressure away from the stage. "Let's go, Hersey. These aren't the usual fans. Let's get out of here before it gets any worse." William's pressure grew steadily as he spoke, he jerked Hersey from the stage and the two of them toppled over in the direction from which they came.

Off-stage now, Glenn toddled back to Hersey's side. She came with a good-natured smile, and it only widened when she saw that her father and god-father had convened so close to the stage. "Is it showtime already?" She grabbed her father's hand and endured a pat on the head from William. Seamlessly, she was accepted into the group's discontent, and her smile faded.

"What in God's name is going on out there?" Hersey shot at William with the intensity of his glare.

"Don't blame me! Those people must've bought up all the tickets before the fans could get to them." William said, gesturing back out to the crowd with a dismissive wave of his hand.

"Heathens." Hersey muttered.

"What?"

"Heathens! They care about Beatrice all of a sudden? I don't think so. No, they're here because they have a thirst to hate anything that tries to bring joy into their meaningless lives." Hersey scowled in the direction of the stage. "I mean, who cares if I have a daughter on a beach in Mexico? She's all grown up. I hardly think that the public has a right to an opinion on whatever habits she may or may not have!" Hersey raised his voice, his jaw trembled and his face turned red to match his eyes.

"She is a James." William said. "It comes with the territory."

"What does that even mean?" Hersey moaned in frustration, and the two of them stewed for a moment.

"I heard she was in pretty bad shape when they found her." William spoke carefully, he waited for a moment of silence to continue onto his next statement. "You can't blame people for worrying about her."

"I care." Glenn tugged on her father's hand from below, and Hersey flinched down as if he'd forgotten all about her. Hersey scraped his daughter's hand away from his own and straightened back up. Taking one big step away from the group, he addressed both Glenn and William as if they were one.

"The show must go on." Hersey's face softened into a stronger sense of certainty. "*The James Gang* doesn't skip episodes, simple as that. Go get Henry, this crowd's gonna need some real warmup before we go on."

"I can't do that to my son." William objected. "They'll eat him alive out there!"

"I'm sorry..." Hersey leaned in closer to his friend. "But maybe you should've thought about that before you got him into the comedy game." He sneered, Glenn stifled a chuckle underneath her breath, and William slouched away to find his son.

"What's so funny?" Hersey asked, noticing the smile that Glenn had lost control of.

"*You're* funny." Glenn chuckled into the hands that were still attempting to cover her lips. Suddenly so childish, she barely managed to get the words out of her mouth before erupting into a fit of giggles. "'*The comedy game*'." Glenn mocked her father with squinting eyes and a comically dignified voice. Hersey could not have been more delighted.

"*Oh*—Maybe we should have you go out there to warm them up if you're such a comedian!" Hersey teased. "Lord knows you'd blow Henry out of the water." He rubbed one of his hands through the scalp of Glenn's hair and dodged her attempts at slapping him away. The two retired to the makeup department.

It wasn't long before the light peaked in its crest through the sky and a bell rang through the nervous hush of the set. High noon meant one thing in the world of *The James Gang*, showtime. With faces caked in makeup, Glenn and Hersey emerged from their booths in tandem. Glenn read her script while Hersey straightened a wrinkle out of his navy blue raincoat. There was always another wrinkle to be straightened, another hair to put in place.

Camera flashes scattered and faded into white noise in the distance. Elroy limped along with the posse of reporters that swarmed the two James's as they approached the stage. Like a storm cloud that hung particularly low in the sky, the reporters had wafted a step behind the James's for the whole morning's journey. Only dissipating when they reached the very edge of the set's allowed access area.

Back at the border of the stage, Hersey and Glenn watched from the side while Henry Elliott—already dressed as Henry James for his coming role in the show— delivered the last ill-received punchline of his stand-up set.

"—I'll save that one for a rainy day!" His voice cracked, and he winced even before the crowd *booed*. Some even threw things down towards the stage. Needless to say, it was the wrong kind of laughter.

"Damned puberty." Hersey muttered with a rare hint of sympathy in his voice. He patted Henry on the back as he exited the stage in shame. "You ready?" He turned to Glenn.

"I'm scared." Glenn pouted.

"Don't be silly." Hersey scoffed and knelt to Glenn's eye-level. "Even *they* wouldn't dare to heckle us when you're on stage. You're America's sweetheart, Glenn. They know that and so should you." Hersey smiled, looking his daughter in the eye. A trepidatious smile came from Glenn in return, and Hersey swept her onto the stage with a yank of her hand.

"*Hersey and Glenn James, everybody!*" The P.A. announcer had to yell into his microphone in order to be heard over the chanting of the crowd.

"*Be-a-trice! Be-a-trice! Be-a-trice!*" The army of young adults rose to their feet, they tore pages out of magazines and threw them down to the stage. The venom was palpable, Hersey bent down and grabbed a page that had landed in-between his feet.

The Daily Dilemma stretched across the top of this cover page in dark red font. The title accompanied a picture of Beatrice, laying prostrated across the sand. She twisted her bikini body away from the paramedic that knelt by her side. Her mouth opened until her jaw reached the end of its capacity, her eyes rolled back towards her skull and her face darkened into a bluish color. It was obvious that she had stepped one foot into a beachy grave by the time the photographer managed to sneak this picture.

"Oh god." Hersey's eyes widened. He noticed the despair that infected Beatrice's eyes, and he shot his attention to the two young figures that approached the stage from the side.

"*Featuring Henry Elliot as Henry James…*" The jeers quieted into more of a rumble than an assault, the crowd had already attacked Henry enough. And besides, they were loading up for the next name. Hersey's stomach plummeted as the P.A.'s voice started back up. "*…and Gretchen Williams as Gretchen James!*"

The crowd's venom kicked into overdrive as Gretchen took her first step out to the exposure of the stage. Her eyes clenched into tight slits, she walked as fast as she could and she forced her lips into a show-business smile. She waved at the crowd and they responded with a barrage of paper airplanes that had been formed from pages of the magazine.

"Imposter!" The Beatrice chant dissipated into a more chaotic kind of outrage when the crowd was faced with the woman who was dressed as her fictional counterpart. Gretchen shifted her weight from one foot to another, fidgeting as she waited for the announcer to cue *The James Gang* into their introductory bow. Fit with a mint green gown that draped underneath a wig of jet-black hair, Gretchen had already gone through her daily transformation into a dead ringer for the real Beatrice James. She had passed the point of no return.

"Wiggins Military Supply presents… The James Gang!" The P.A. announcer pumped a fist in the air to prompt a bow from the cast. Canned applause erupted from the stage's speakers and mixed in with the overwhelming sound of the crowd's unrest. The canned applause shifted into the show's opening theme, and network television's first family fled to the side of the stage.

TV screens lit up all around the auditorium, the room got dark and the projections rolled with the show's opening credits. "What's going on out there?" Henry demanded an answer from his father, who was too busy adjusting his son's sleeves to offer anything more than a noncommittal grunt.

"They're mad at me." Hersey admitted. Socked into a single off-stage prep room with every one of his co-stars milling about at once, he was feeling quite open. "They're mad at me because I'm still here while Beatrice is suffering on a beach in Mexico." Hersey reached into the pocket of his raincoat and came out with the magazine cover that he'd collected from the stage. "They don't understand that my real family's right here with me. I'm just sorry they're taking it out on you." Hersey smiled softly. He extended a hand to place on Gretchen's shoulder, but she jerked away from his reach.

"You wouldn't let them treat family like this." Gretchen's voice cracked, she was bordering on tears. Glenn whimpered in the corner of the room and the rest of *The James Gang* fell into silence.

"I'll tell you what—" Hersey said, staring at the face on the magazine as he demanded the attention of his co-stars. "If you can power through this recording, if you can dig deep and deal with those hoodlums, then I'll take the show on the road to Mexico next week." The room remained silent, blank stares searched for something within Hersey's eyes. "Then we can see Beatrice! We'll get her to go on the show, she'll let the world know that she's fine, and then these delinquents will have to give us a break!" Hersey smiled with a hint of desperation.

"What makes you so sure she's okay?" Gretchen asked, her voice was shrill and tired from months of weekly performances without a break. Her meager voice strained, but the hoarseness made it easy for Hersey to ignore.

Another bell sounded, it screamed through the hallways and banged in through the door to the prep room. The music quieted outside, and the *boos* unearthed themselves from the cover of the extra noise. "They sure aren't tiring themselves out." William winced when he heard the bell.

"Then it's agreed." Hersey clapped and pushed himself up from his seat to take a more powerful stance. "Let's get through this together. As a family!"

Gretchen rolled her eyes. As the oldest of the child actors on *The James Gang*, she'd adopted a sense of cynicism when it came to her belief in compromise. Hersey's way or the highway, that's how things had been for the past nine seasons, and Gretchen saw no reason to believe that things were changing now. She grunted as she followed the rest of the actors back to the stage.

The opening theme's final guitar riff rang into the back of the auditorium before fading into a moment of unobstructed *booing*. Glenn sat in between Gretchen and Henry, the three of them milled about in their make-believe Mexico. The light came back into focus on the stage and Hersey stepped forward into the view of the crowd. "There you are!" Hersey always raised his voice into a slightly higher register when he was performing. "I've been looking all over for you kids, why did you run away from me?"

"Henry saw a great white shark waving at him, and we're building a boat to go catch it!" Glenn also heightened the octave of her voice on stage. It was a habit inherited from her father, no doubt. Not that she needed any help sounding like a child.

"*Shhh!*" Henry forced his head into his acting-sister's field of vision. "That was supposed to be our secret!"

"Secrets, secrets, are no fun. Secrets, secrets, hurt someone." Glenn went back to her preoccupation with the sand.

Gretchen chimed in, lounging in the sand and tanning herself under the fake rays of the sun. "That's not what you told me when you had that little mishap on the plane ride over here!"

All the actors waited. Canned laughter began to pour in from the edges of the stage, but it was quickly overtaken by a thunder of *boos* that drowned the punchline and stomped it into the submission of an excruciating death.

The rest of the show was an exercise in straining to be heard over the negative energy in the crowd. Security guards lined the edge of the stage and deflected most, but not all, of the paper airplanes. Nothing could be done to help the noise, the chants and insults were worse than any opposing crowd at a sporting event (even a Philidelphian one), and the projectiles were much more psychologically challenging than a tub of popcorn or a stray cup of soda.

Hersey's face had become so stark in its embarrassed redness that he refused his usual ritual of watching the show back immediately after recording. He stormed through the backstage area with a huff. Without a word to share with any of his co-stars, Hersey disappeared into the trailer that he shared with Glenn. He snapped the door locked when she tried to follow him inside. Little Glenn banged on the door, her ponytail was too tight and her swimsuit was itchy from performing under the harsh stage lighting. She slammed her hands against the hardwood, but only heard one word in return to her plea through the door. "No... No... No..."

Hersey spoke his chant through a voice that muffled against the padding on the trailer's side wall. He braced himself against the other side of the door that Glenn banged on and he melted more weight into his resistance each time Glenn yelled to be let in.

William was the next to show up. "Hersey?" He moved Glenn off to the left so he could assume the central position on that side of the door. William knocked in light spurts, he only extended one knuckle when he went to hit the door and the sound he made was something akin to that of a leaky faucet's drip. It wasn't long before the door swung back open.

"My *God*, would you stop knocking like that?" Hersey leaned out from his trailer to face both William and Glenn. Glenn scampered past her father, she squirted in through a gap between Hersey's leg and the side of the doorframe, she disappeared into her changing area and sighed with relief.

"Tough day at work?" William smiled and took a step backwards. "Can I come in?"

"No." Hersey pouted for a moment before stepping out of his trailer to join his director on even-ground. "Happy now?"

"Hardly." William said, his smile faded into the kind that can't be seen beyond your lips. "The people are *not* happy with you."

"*Oh*, you said it yourself!" Hersey scrunched his face into a ball of disgust. "Those weren't our fans, they were the product of a juvenile detention center from hell!" Hersey flung a sarcastic finger back in the direction of the stage. "I'm gonna have one hell of a talk with the booking department about *that* field trip. I swear to God."

"I saw some familiar faces in there, Hersey. There were more than a couple adults in that crowd. Adults become parents and we're in real trouble if the parents are out there *booing* us on stage like that."

"You sound like a producer." Hersey groaned. "Where's Mr. Wiggins hiding? After all, it is his money we're risking here, isn't it?" Hersey smiled, holding his mouth open while he paused for a moment to dwell on his rebuttal. "And don't act like you were out there with us today." Hersey stepped backwards, back into the trailer and away from William, he shut the door behind him and collapsed his weight back up against the door. "And Will?" Hersey raised his voice through the now closed door that separated them.

"Hersey?" William had been about to turn away.

"We leave for Mexico tomorrow morning. Bright and early, don't be late."

A smile cracked into William's face and he completed his turn away from the trailer. "Sounds good, *boss*." He was late to drop Henry off at his mother's house on the way home that day.

"Well Glenn, how's Mexico sound?" Hersey unzipped his raincoat and tipped his beret back so his forehead could breathe. "You wanted to see Beatrice, you're gonna get your wish tomorrow morning. I'd say you're welcome, but I don't believe that I've been properly thanked yet." He sat at a booth that stretched along the side of the trailer and waited for Glenn to emerge from her changing area.

Glenn came out in pajamas, a head-to-toe assortment of *James Gang* logos and designs that draped her body in light cotton fabric. Bags formed and shadowed the bottoms of her eyes, and she slouched as if she were dripping into the cracks in the floor. "I'm sorry, dad." Glenn pinched at her scalp and sniffled as she spoke.

"Hey—" Hersey leaned down to Glenn's eye-level to be a better comfort. "Let's leave this all behind. One bad night can't hurt us, can it? I mean, how weak are we if we let a couple *boos* kill us like that? Let's leave this all behind, Glenn. Let's head south with a new lease on life!" Hersey raised his thumb for a playful flick at the chin of his youngest daughter. Glenn had the thinnest lips that Hersey had ever seen, and they peeled into a smile.

"We're off to rescue Beatrice! We're off to rescue Beatrice!" Glenn sang as she burst out the doors of the trailer. With one hand charging ahead and holding a make-believe sword, the other flapped behind her and sent her skipping through the air. She blew past Henry and his father. "Haven't you heard the good news?" She'd skipped by before they had a chance to answer her. She hummed "Lovely Day" by Bill Withers and she closed her eyes as she skipped all the way back to her father's Jaguar XJS.

Glenn didn't sleep well that night. She rolled the length of her bed from end-to-end and back again, she brimmed with energy that simply would not confine her to the mattress. Beatrice's picture flashed in and out of Glenn's mind. She'd only caught a glimpse of her sister's cover-page back in the prep room, one look was more than enough.

After hours of unrest, a knock came as a relief to Glenn. She'd been writhing around in bed for so long by that time that any distraction would have been preferable to the insomnia. She hated the silence of a sleepless night. Glenn grunted to verbalize the fact that she was still awake, and the door creaked further open. Hersey appeared within the crack. "You up, kid?"

"Yeah." Glenn pulled the covers down and sat up in bed, an action she'd been thinking about doing for hours. "I can't sleep."

"Neither can I." Hersey walked over and sat down at the foot of Glenn's bed. "No James has ever been able to sleep the night before a trip, it's just not our way."

"What do you mean?"

"Your grandfather Scruffy James was famous for cleaning the *whole* house the night before we went anywhere. He'd be up all night; sweeping, dusting, polishing and organizing everything that he could get his hands on. He got so good at it that nobody would want to leave by the time he was done cleaning!" Hersey smiled, and his story got a giggle out of Glenn. She followed his lead when he got up from bed. "It's not in our blood. We James's are homebodies, your sisters are a good example of what happens when we leave the nest."

Glenn stepped in her father's footsteps as the two James's walked into the foyer of the *James Gang* mansion. "Now—" Hersey straightened up. "We were much less fortunate in those days, and old Scruffy didn't exactly have this much space to clean back then." Hersey paused next to one of the many closets that lined the foyer's back wall. He smiled, and reached in for a broom. "But even we must leave some times, and tradition is tradition. Isn't it, Glenn?"

By now, the sleep had completely washed out from Glenn's eyes. She smiled wildly when she accepted the broom and she darted around the room as soon as she could. She pushed the broom in front of her as if it were a hockey player's stick. "This is better than tossing and turning all night. Isn't it, Glenn?" Hersey yelled as he bent down to inspect his crate of records for the proper soundtrack. *Wings Over America*, the sound of Paul McCartney's voice poured out of the record player's speaker and filled the whole mansion with the rattly echo of its sound.

Glenn sped up now that she had the music to propel her in her cleaning. She swept circles around Hersey in the foyer, she charged her broom across the red marble staircases and tore up and down every hallway that she could find within the maze of a mansion. The youngest

James was really giving Scruffy a run for his money. The sun snuck in between the cracks in the shades that covered the mansion's windows and—although it would have taken heaven and earth to stop Glenn from wanting to go to Mexico—the mansion was spotless by the time Hersey called for her to meet him by the front door.

"Is it time to go already?" Glenn asked. She walked down the stairs to the front door, her face was red and shining with the sweat of a hard morning's work.

"Time flies, doesn't it?" Hersey smirked, the bags were packed and he shook his foot against the ground as if he were getting nervous about something. "You can thank your grandfather for that trick, it works every time." Hersey handed a backpack off to Glenn, he settled her with two handbags, a purse and another tote bag, before walking out the door with two free hands.

Outside, the air's heat turned distant objects into wavy lines that fluctuated in Glenn's vision as she climbed into the backseat of Hersey's car. Glenn sighed as she sat down and Hersey slapped her with a light hand on her back. "You better get used to this sun, it's gonna be a lot more of the same when we're in Mexico." Hersey was beaming. He stared into the sun as he climbed into the driver's seat, and he chuckled to himself as he started the car's engine. Glenn thought of Beatrice on the ride to the airport. Hersey chuckled in the front seat, and he brought the car to a halt far earlier than Glenn had been expecting.

"Dad?" Glenn prompted her father. They had screeched to a stop in front of some kind of government building where large groups of people stood and chanted, holding signs in protest of some foreign war. Hersey swung his feet out of the car before answering.

"Gotta make a quick stop, won't be long now." He left, Glenn twisted around to watch while her father disappeared into the crowd of unrest. Young people screaming and chanting their faces off, they reminded Glenn of the faces that she'd seen in the crowd at the latest recording of *The James Gang*. She wondered if these were the same people that had screamed in her father's face only a day before, she wondered if they could see her through the tinted window of the car.

Hersey reappeared before too long, just long enough for Glenn to start worrying, really. He came back out of the crowd with a familiar face hanging off of his arm, he limped along with Hersey and stumbled around for a bit before climbing into the passenger's seat. "Hey kid!" Elroy Bartholomew leaned around the back of his seat to face Glenn. He stared with a reporter's admiration in his eyes.

"What're you doing here?" Glenn asked. She'd been patient, but the adults laughed the way some adults do when they want to dismiss a perfectly valid question because it's coming from a high pitched voice.

"Elroy's gonna help document our trip, Glenn." Hersey was still chuckling, he nodded towards Elroy and smiled as if he were apologizing for the curiosity of his daughter. The two men swooned in tandem, they sighed as if they were honeymooning to Paris, they sighed as if one had not run over the other's toe just a day before.

"Is he gonna help us find Beatrice?" Glenn asked and her father rolled his eyes.

"Yes, Glenn. He's gonna help us find Beatrice." Glenn smiled in a half measure. It was rare for her to smile without beaming in a manner that contorted her entire face. This time, her smile tugged at one corner of one lip, and it stopped at that.

"Don't you worry about a thing!" Elroy tapped Glenn on her knee and darted a smile back and forth between her and Hersey. "We'll get your sister back on track in no time." Elroy winked, Hersey got onto the highway and Elroy turned his attention back to the driver. "And I'll be covering the whole thing like CCTV at a bank!" Elroy laughed and playfully hit Hersey on the shoulder. "Get it?"

"Oh yeah, I gotcha." Hersey laughed a plastic kind of laugh. "'*CCTV*', that's a good one."

The airport was cold, someone had overcompensated for the outside's heatwave by cranking the thermostat into the negatives. Glenn shivered and groaned as she walked. Thankfully, Elroy was nice enough to take some of the bags off of her hands, but Hersey was no help. It's surprisingly hard for a five year old to shiver and lift at the same time.

Hersey was bombarded by fans that couldn't recognize Glenn behind her stacks of luggage. He signed autographs and kissed babies all the way over to the boarding area where William and the rest of the crew waited—also being bombarded by the buzzing gibberish of the fans—for their arrival.

William looked like he'd seen a ghost, and he stormed forward to meet Hersey, Glenn, and Elroy, before they got a chance to settle in at the gate. The rest of the crew began to board the plane. Glenn and Elroy went ahead, but William planted his hands onto Hersey's shoulders, stopping him in his tracks. "I have to talk to you." William spoke with a voice that leaked air like a *hiss*. His head bowed and his thumbs lowered to fidget around in his pockets. He was struggling to speak.

"Isn't this more like it?" Hersey ignored the look that William had on his face. "I told you that we shouldn't be worrying about our fans. I mean, from the looks of it, they've come back with a vengeance!" Hersey raised his voice and the crowd responded with an obligatory *roar* of support.

"Hersey—" William's sorrow intensified to a point beyond Hersey's ability to ignore.

"What's bothering you?" Hersey's smile faded and the surrounding fans fell into an anxious kind of silence. Hersey was quick to paste a new smile over the top of his old one when he remembered that he had an audience for this conversation. "This is a great day, Will. What could be bothering you on a great day like today?" Hersey gritted his teeth to illuminate the joy that he was intent on portraying.

It took a few more moments of silence for Hersey to fill in the blanks that William could not seem to offer with words. "Should we speak on the plane?" The expectant crowd groaned, William nodded with a neck that hung like a zombie, and Hersey guided his shell-shocked director through the gate.

"Okay." William finally exhaled when he sat down in a seat next to Hersey. New York to Cabo San Lucas, the flight was stuffed to the brim with members of *The James Gang's* extended family—that's what Hersey liked to call crew members and extras that came back more than once or twice.

"Okay?" Hersey egged William on when he fell back into silence.

"Yes—" William straightened his back in his seat. "It's about Beatrice, it's—" He was stuttering now. "It's *The Dilemma*. They lost her!"

William's face froze as if paralyzed in fear. It was an honest fear, one that rooted itself firmly in concern for Beatrice's well-being, though he dreaded Hersey's response in equal measure. He feared the words he was saying and it held him in silence, there was and would never be any elaboration. Not until Hersey proved his ability to take this well.

"Well, good for her." Hersey snapped a bag of complementary peanuts open in his lap. "It gave me a queasy kinda feeling that Elroy's minions were swarming around her like that. She hasn't exactly been a friend to the show in the past, you know? I didn't like the idea of her getting all that air time."

"I don't think you understand—"

"What is there to understand, William? Why don't you just tell me what you're after instead of making me guess at it?" Hersey talked through a mouthful of peanuts. "Now we won't get scooped!" An unintentional chunk of peanut flew from Hersey's lip onto the crest of William's chin. Though William's repulsion had started long before the peanut landed.

"Right." William said. He sighed as he scraped the chunk away from his face. "Well they were the only ones who had her location. They were willing to share her with us and now they've lost her. Just in case you care."

Just then, Hersey stood up in his seat. He widened his eyes and whipped his head around. He looked for Glenn, and when he found her, playing alone in her seat near the back of the plane, he sat back down. "*Don't* tell Glenn." Hersey leaned closer to William's face, his breath reeked of peanuts and his jaw hardened into the shape of a square. "I mean it."

William nodded, and they spent the rest of the flight in silence.

Glenn woke herself up with a yell that coincided with the bump of the plane's wheels as they touched down for a landing. "Mexico!" She yelled, and the noise shook the rest of the plane into a higher register of alertness. While the crew murmured and stretched around Hersey and William, Glenn rushed to the front of the plane to reunite with her father.

"Are we there, dad? Did we make it to Mexico?" Glenn bounced in the aisle, crewmembers squeezed by while Glenn tugged at her the collar of her father's coat.

"I'd say that's a pretty good bet, my darling." Hersey yawned and stretched before waking the sleeping William that snored beside him. Glenn bounced and celebrated the landing with a subtle dance as Hersey began stacking bags in his daughter's hands. Elroy mosied over to their seat after the rest of the passengers had disembarked. His face was gaunt and pale, having made great use of his seat's barf bag, he walked as if he was ten pounds lighter.

"That was one hell of a babysitting job your boys did!" William said. "I couldn't have lost her quicker if I tried!" Everybody snapped towards William now, Glenn's eyes widened and William sank back into his seat. He covered his mouth with both of his hands.

"Who did you lose?" Glenn turned to Elroy and asked her question from behind a growing stack of luggage.

"I don't know. William, who *did* we lose?" Elroy turned both his and Glenn's attention towards William.

"Just a cruel joke, my dear. Grown-up stuff." Hersey stepped in before Glenn got too suspicious, he gently scratched his daughter on the shoulder before pushing her into a pivot towards the plane's cockpit. "Why don't you go up there and thank the pilot for landing us safely, huh?" Hersey smiled. "I'm sure it would give him a kick to see America's sweetheart in *real life*, don't you think that's a good idea?"

"You really think *he* would want to see me?" Glenn bounced up and down on her toes, she said the word *'he'* the way some people refer to God. Hersey nodded and Glenn raced to the front of the plane.

Hersey's face darkened now that Glenn was occupied by the pilot. He stood up, his lanky torso stretched towards the ceiling and encapsulated both William and Elroy within his shadow. "She does *not* hear about this." He pointed towards the front of the plane. "She *cannot* hear about this." Hersey frowned, shaking his head, he walked off in silence.

Hersey scooped Glenn away from the pilot as he exited the plane. Glenn wiggled her way away from his grasp before too long, but she grabbed at Hersey's slacks every once in a while as a way to check in.

There was a tall man waiting for them when they entered the airport. "Hersey James?" The man was far too pale to have been in Mexico for any extended period of time. He held a sign with Hersey's name scrawled in cursive and he spoke in a high pitch that tuned everything he said into a question.

"That's me, what do you want?" Hersey grunted when he saw his name on the man's sign. Visibly caught off guard, his voice came off more abrasive than he'd intended.

"This is for you." The man said. He slipped a folded piece of paper from his jacket pocket into Hersey's, he tried to whisper but his high voice gave him away. He turned and walked away before Hersey could ask any of the questions that appeared in his head.

"What is this?" Hersey looked up and asked his question to the air, the strange man was already too far to hear him. Hersey looked down and looked at Glenn. Bewildered, he shook his head.

"What is that?" Glenn asked.

"I didn't know we were getting anything." Hersey paused to look up, he looked towards the space where the strange pale man had disappeared from. "Hell, I've been to Mexico about ten times on *The James Gang*, but never in real life. I can't think of anyone who'd even know we were coming."

"Open it!" Glenn yelled and Hersey flinched. Rearing for a mystery, Glenn clapped her hands and started running loosely in place. "Open it!" She repeated. Hersey turned his back to his daughter and started to open the letter. He read the note with Glenn kicking at his calves in protest. "I wanna see!" She cried as she kicked, but Hersey was too focused on his reading to notice.

The letter made its words by using a variety of clippings from pages of magazines. Hersey even recognized a few of the pastings from Beatrice's cover article in *The Daily Dilemma*. Noticeably, Beatrice's name was the only word that had been spelled out in a single clipping. "Beatrice James" had been lifted right from her cover in big, blocky letters.

"*URGENT: Meet me at the corner booth of Loomis's Spirits on the waterfront. Come during happy hour. Come alone if you ever want to see Beatrice James again.*" The letter was over glued, letters sank on the page and any of the words could've been scrambled around like magnets on a refrigerator. It took Hersey a minute or two to even make sense of the words he was reading, he was quick to stuff the paper back into his pocket when he did.

"What does it say?" Glenn lifted onto her tiptoes as Hersey turned back around to face her.

"Nothing you should worry about." Hersey dismissed the question, only continuing when Glenn gave him a skeptical look. "It's business. Rights that'll allow us to film on the beach when we get to that sister of yours!" Hersey smiled and Glenn followed suit. She tugged at the bottom of her father's raincoat, and his face darkened when William and Elroy caught up to the group.

The four of them walked a good distance behind the larger pack of the extended *James Gang* family. The adults spoke in hushed tones, and Glenn practiced her dance moves in front of them. "Beatrice could get shipped to China tomorrow for all I care!" Hersey exclaimed his words, but Glenn was too focused to notice. She waltzed by herself, grasping hands and clinging bodies with the air. Hersey quieted down for the next part. "As long as she's on the show before then, I really couldn't care less."

"I assume this is off the record." Elroy smirked, and Hersey's face hardened. William's eyes had grown hollow and his face turned green at the sound of Hersey's hate.

"You know, you were so quiet on that plane ride that I almost forgot you were a snake! I can remove access just as easily as I can give it, remember that." Hersey sneered at Elroy before peeling away from the group with William. "So what're we gonna do?" Hersey whispered, hypervigilant now that Elroy caught him in a rant.

"Well, you've gotta meet this guy if you want to keep her safe. My God, who knows what they're doing to poor

Beatrice. I'm sorry, Hersey, but I don't think we have any other options here."

"What about Glenn?"

"You're her dad."William shrugged, he held the exit door open for Hersey to walk through. "I'm gonna be as honest with Henry as possible. But Glenn, she's a different creature."

"I know." Hersey sighed as he got into the car that was waiting for them outside the airport. "She's too damn pure for this stuff!" Hersey paused, Glenn climbed into the car seat behind Hersey and William, and Hersey lowered his voice. He whispered into William's ear. "Keep her busy while I'm gone, will ya?" He nudged William on his shoulder and William started the car.

The James Gang's extended family infested their hotel like rats at a buffet. Fit with navy blue raincoats to match Hersey's, their job was only identifiable through the color of the stocking cap on their head. Purple for extras, various shades of red for the crew. Hersey couldn't walk five steps without being thanked for the trip, or for the job, or for the way that he smiled at them on their first day of filming. Hersey offered the same warm nod for every response. His graciousness— much like his autograph—had become so ingrained that he hardly even had to force his smile anymore.

Hersey dropped Glenn off at William's room before reversing course and returning to the lobby. There Elroy waited, running both hands through his hair, entranced by the reflection that he caught in the metallic door of the elevator. "You wanted to see me?" Elroy's vanity turned into nonchalance when Hersey stepped into view in the lobby.

"Do you have your camera?" Hersey smiled, he seemed giddy in a way that was more genuine than the panic he exuded in the airport. Elroy hated actors for this exact reason, most of them are still acting when the cameras turn off. Elroy nodded and pulled a camera out from his bag. "You won't need it yet." Hersey waved him off. "Do you have your notepad?"

"You're awfully excited to talk to—what was I? A snake?" Elroy frowned as he lifted a notepad out from the bottom of his bag.

"You don't need that yet either." Hersey waved him off again. "When did I call you a snake?"

"In the airport."

"With William around?" Hersey's face lit into a smirk, the corner of his lip buried itself inside of the smile line on his cheek. "Oh Elroy, I thought you knew better than this! You saw William's face when I ranted about needing Beatrice for the show, he was horrified!" Hersey did all he could to keep from laughing. "He's a weak one when it comes to the media, always has been."

"So you called me a snake?" Elroy followed Hersey's lead and the two of them got back into the car.

"I said what William needed to hear." Hersey finally laughed as he started to drive. "I need him almost as much as I need you, you know. After all, what's all the publicity for if we don't have a TV special for the culmination?" Hersey lowered his voice. "I'm talking about 24/7 access to the greatest event in television history here. I'm talking about the future of television!" That coaxed a smile from Elroy, then the car took a left and stopped along the waterfront.

Loomis's Spirits was not an unknown quantity in the life of Hersey James. He recognized that old pirate ship wood as if it were the warmer side of his pillow, and he

walked through the bar's entrance as if he were back in
New York, anxious for a welcome from a room of friendly
faces. Hersey came into his local Loomis's on a nightly
basis. On some days, that was his only excursion into
the world outside of the *James Gang* mansion. People
exhausted Hersey, people in Loomis's Spirits, however,
had the opposite effect.

"Red wine, whatever's your best." Hersey breezed by
the bar. He tapped his fingers along the counter and hardly
made eye-contact with the bartender before redirecting his
attention towards the corners of the room.

"Make that two." Elroy followed up. Signaling two
fingers at the bartender, he animated as if speaking a
foreign language. He caught up just in time to hear the
return of Hersey's voice.

"There." Hersey nudged his chin in the direction of
the darkest and furthest corner of the bar. "You see that?"
A woman tapped a manicured fingernail that wrapped
around a newspaper that was covering her face. "Get your
camera ready and don't get too close, I want you to get all
of this."

Hersey snatched both glasses of wine while Elroy bent
down to get his camera. Hersey was halfway over to the
corner booth by the time Elroy stood back up. He sighed.
"Can I get another?" He asked, and the bartender nodded
as Elroy sat down and flashed an inconspicuous picture at
the corner of the room.

"Care for a drink?" Hersey asked, he extended one of
his two glasses towards the corner booth. The newspaper
lowered just below the woman's eyes. She was wearing
a heavy knit cap that seemed to be covering an unruly
mound of hair. It was crocheted baby blue and yellow,

and she peered in a way that confirmed her recognition of something on the other side of her prop paper.

"Sit down." The person's voice came as the newspaper lowered the rest of the way down to her lap. The voice was low and full of bass. The newspaper folded neatly into her lap, and she looked up to show her face in the bar's dim light. "Hello Hersey!"

Kitty James folded her hands across her chest and smiled a superior kind of smile. Hersey's head flew back in shock, and he just about flung himself from the booth when he heard the next *click* that came from Elroy's camera. Kitty followed her father's gaze and immediately noticed the man that was trying to be inconspicuous with his camera on his hip at the bar. "Kitty." Hersey's voice wobbled as he straightened himself back up in his seat. He spoke louder than usual, all the better to distract Kitty from the cameraman. The best pictures are always the candids, anyways. "*I*—I assume you brought me here. Didn't you?"

"Either that or this is all some kind of worldwide coincidence." Kitty laughed, she rumbled the wine glasses with the depth of her voice, and Hersey's confusion faded to a frown.

"You know, I've seen just about every wicked trick in the book; from you, from your sister, for the past twenty years; but this, this is a whole new level! The blackmail, the lying! My dear, you've become the black sheep of all black sheep!"

Kitty waited for an excruciating moment before responding to her father. She replaced the cigarette that burnt over one end of her mouth and used the other to sip from her wine. She winced. "That's terrible, I would've expected some better taste from *you* of all people." Kitty said '*you*' as if she'd personally watched while Hersey drank the entirety of The E. & J. Gallo Winery's stock. "And who said anything about lying?" She swallowed.

"What would you call it?"

"Escape!" Kitty smiled, flashed another glance into the camera, and took a bigger sip from her wine. "But you wouldn't know anything about that since you've embraced your mouse trap with such open arms." She tipped her head to acknowledge that Elroy's cover was blown, she smiled.

"You call it escape? That's close, I call it extortion."

"Extortion of what? You don't have a single thing that I want, and you never will." Kitty waited, holding her breath as if she had to stop herself from erupting with words. "There is no lie, there is no extortion—"

"Then why am I here?" Hersey interrupted, his exasperation seemed to irk the zen that Kitty was forcing.

"What if I wanted you to know that your daughter is safe, is that so hard for you to imagine?" Kitty's face was getting red. "Beatrice is safe and she prefers *my* care, is that so hard for you to imagine?"

"Who could you possibly care for?" Hersey guffawed. Leaning back in his chair, he downed his wine in a single sip.

"I'm much better now." Kitty lowered her eyes to the table, she softened her voice as she spoke. "Haven't you noticed?"

"Honestly?" Hersey laughed. "You've terrified me since the day you spilled out!."

"I'm *better now*!" Kitty raised her voice and cracked a fist against the table. She frowned at Hersey, and a scornful tear beaded near the edge of her eyelid.

"Well, obviously." Hersey exaggerated a flinch while Kitty got up, he watched while her hands turned to fists.

"Look how calm you've become!" Kitty seethed as Hersey reached across the table for the other glass. "You're not gonna drink this?" He tipped the glass toward his seat and inspected the contents. And just then, Kitty slammed a hand onto Hersey's wrist to stop him from dragging it away.

"Mine." Kitty could hardly form the word through her gritted teeth.

"That's fine." Hersey waited for Kitty to relax her grip. And just when she did, he jerked the glass over to his side of the table. "Mine!" He exclaimed, using his best impression of Kitty's deep voice.

Hersey laughed, Kitty did not. She pounced across the table and extended both hands to her father's neck. She latched on and squeezed. "All better, huh?" Hersey squealed as he tried to wiggle away from his middle daughter's chokehold. Hersey's bloodstained eyes darkened and his face began to purple.

Just as Hersey's breath was about to squeeze to a complete shut, just as he began to resign himself to an oxygen-less existence, a woman in bug-eyed sunglasses sprang from her seat at a neighboring booth.

"It's not worth it, *he's* not worth it, it's not worth it, *he's* not worth it." Hersey came back to lucidity with the sound of this chant. His blurry vision inched back into focus, and the ringing quieted from his ears. Hersey was still seeing double when he came to. "It's not worth it, *he's* not worth it." The higher pitched voice removed the doubt from his mind.

"Glenn, you followed us?"

"Think again." The voice stopped chanting long enough to respond. Hersey's vision cleared the rest of the way and he saw her.

"Beatrice!" Hersey celebrated, and his confusion subsided. "Oh I absolutely *must* talk to you." Hersey smiled at his daughters, though neither of them was smiling back.

"Why's that?" Beatrice asked, still holding Kitty in place as she struggled to calm down.

"*Why*—Maybe because the entire Western hemisphere is worried about you!" Hersey finished Kitty's wine before turning his attention back towards the bar. "Elroy!" He called, beckoning the reporter to a seat next to himself. "*Ah*, reinforcements." Hersey smiled as Elroy took a seat. "We want the world to know that you're okay!"

"Oh yeah, and what if there's a reason I disappeared?" Beatrice sneered, particularly focusing her ire on Elroy. "What if *you* suffocated me with your cameras and your questions? What if I didn't have any other choice?"

The group fell silent, every eye in the bar was falling on Elroy. Even the needles were waiting to drop, they were dying to hear what he had to say. Elroy folded a napkin and laid it gently onto his lap, his eyes gave his ignorance away long before he said a word.

"Everybody's got a job to do." Elroy smiled a polite smile with lips that met only lightly to cover his teeth.

"Why is he here?" Kitty had calmed enough to speak, her face was still red though the tears had left her eyes. She faced Hersey with a blank stare, only briefly motioning towards Elroy before refocusing on her father.

"Like I said—" Hersey folded his hands on top of the table. "We were *all* very worried."

"Was the camera as worried as you were?" Kitty raised her voice, both Elroy and Hersey flinched and Beatrice snickered at the fear on their faces.

"That thing really follows you around. It's like a puppy, isn't it?" Beatrice added. She was calmer than her sister, but her disdain was really starting to shine through. "Why bring a camera? I mean, isn't it enough to save your daughter without documenting the whole thing?"

"Well apparently you never needed saving in the first place, so I guess we'll never know." Hersey raised his voice to match Kitty's, but he didn't look into a single pair of eyes when he did it. He was distracted, waving at the bartender for another glass of wine.

"It does matter!" Beatrice relented. The last one to raise her voice, she got shrill around her second word. "We ran away for a little piece of mind. I damn near had to force Kitty to reach out to you with that letter, and you brought the enemy right along with you! I should have expected as much." Beatrice *hissed* her words. She settled back in the seat and folded her arms over a deep-breathing chest. She was hurt, and for the briefest of moments, in the bar's dimmest light, she looked exactly like Glenn.

Hersey and Elroy conferred in silence at the other end of the booth, they darted their glances and shifted their eyebrows and did everything they could to try to coax the other one into speaking first. Hersey lost the staring contest, and he treaded very lightly when he finally started to speak. "*I*—I guess there won't be any *good* time to ask you this…" Hersey stuttered, the bartender gave him his drink and he downed it in another grapey gulp.

"Might as well get it over with then." Beatrice's ire was leaning towards exhaustion by then.

Hersey examined his hand against the base of his wine glass. "We wanted you to come on for the next episode. Just for a little bit, just so the world knows that you're okay." Hersey raised his eyebrows towards his daughter. The bartender had barely made his way back to the bar before having to turn around, he delivered another glass of wine to Hersey's seat.

"You what?" Beatrice doubled over. Caught halfway between hysteria and homicide, she gasped.

"We want you to come on the show." Hersey's speech gained confidence as he spoke. "We brought the whole extended family down to Mexico and everything." He smiled and Beatrice crossed her arms.

"I hate that you call them that." She spat, tightening her grip around her chest. "It makes it sound so easy to be a James, like all you have to do is tell a few jokes in front of the camera or something. They don't know what it's like to be a *real* James, they don't know what it's like when those camera's refuse to turn off." She was staring at Elroy again. Kitty was starting to stir in her seat, but Beatrice was quick to plant her back into the booth.

"And you don't know what it's like to be on the show." Hersey smirked. Leaning back in his seat, he was well aware of the tempers that were flaring in front of him.

"Think of this as an opportunity." Elroy was half sarcastic when he interjected. Talking to Beatrice while smirking at Kitty's frown, he whipped his camera out and flashed a quick picture. They flinched. "You'll finally get your chance to duke it out with Gretchen on national TV!" Elroy flashed another picture before retiring his camera back into his bag. Kitty blinked.

The bar got quiet again, only the bartender lingered long enough to spectate this far, and he had been properly silenced by the spectacle. Three A-list celebrities in one booth, all boiling towards a breaking point that was sure to erupt. Beatrice took a couple blank blinks into Elroy's eyes before leaning back in her seat and reapplying her black hole circular sunglasses. She took a deep breath and looked to the side where Kitty was ticking back and forth like a timebomb. "Let's go." Beatrice said. She leaned over the table as if she were going to shake her father's hand, but she grabbed his wine glass instead.

"*Aargh!*" Hersey screamed. Wine sloshed from his cup and into both eyes before he had a chance to react. He cupped them, pressed against them with his palms, and flailed in his seat. Forever inexplicably irritated, Hersey's eyes glowed red as he tried to blink the rest of the wine away. Beatrice held Kitty's hand and pulled her away from the booth, Kitty cackled and the two of them walked out of the bar.

"We should stop them, shouldn't we?" Elroy said, not looking at Hersey, who was straining and vigorously rubbing his eyes.

"Of course we should!" Hersey peeled himself up to look at Elroy, the rubbing had turned his skin red and he screamed at Elroy with a raccoon's mask of irritation around his eyes. Elroy hesitated for a moment of astonishment before Hersey snapped and kicked him into action. "*Go, Go, Go!*" The two scrambled out the door in chase.

Clear sky struck Hersey's eyes and immediately blinded him to the world outside of the dimly lit bar. He lagged behind Elroy, feeling the air in front of him as if his hands were antennae telling him which direction to walk. "There!" Elroy shouted. He flashed a picture at the corner and ran, crossing the street and leaving Hersey to scramble around in his dust.

"You see them?" Hersey stumbled up against the pole of a streetlight. "I'll be right there." He was blinking as fast as he could, but his vision's improvement was incremental at best. He heard discussion in the distance, it was calm but still far away. He blinked more, he kneeled down on the sidewalk to better retain his balance. The voices seemed like they were approaching.

"Not much of an athlete these days, are you?" A deep voice was halfway cackling when it approached the cowering celebrity.

"Not many athletes are blinded during pregame warmups." Hersey completed his stumble back onto his feet. Still rapidly blinking, his vision was finally starting to clear up. Hersey blinked one more hard time to see that Kitty and Beatrice had returned with Elroy by their side. "*Wh*—" Hersey smiled and Kitty rolled her eyes. "You girls had a change of heart?"

"Forgot my purse." Beatrice didn't even break her stride as she walked past her father to re-enter the bar. A moment of awkward silence passed, Hersey feared Kitty's wraith and Kitty wasn't in the mood to spark any smalltalk while her sister was retrieving her purse. Beatrice re-emerged after about a minute spent inside.

"No purse?" Kitty was the one to break the silence.

"No purse. I swear I had it in there." Beatrice sighed. She flinched at the feeling of a strong hand's placement on her shoulder. Hersey had grabbed her, desperate tears dried around the corners of his eyes.

"*Please.*" Hersey pleaded with a shake in his voice. "*Please, Glenn's desperate to know you're alright, she really hasn't been herself since you started your run on infamy. She's sick with worry about you. She's withering and sick, her blonde has gone black and her voice has gone raspy. Your return might just be her last hope!*" Hersey howled, and Beatrice pried his hand from her shoulder. Not yet completely disaffected, she frowned when she heard the sound of Glenn's name.

"Really?" Beatrice's eyes widened beyond the point of most human possibility.

"Yes." Hersey forced his face into a real paternal smile. Elroy snickered silently in the background, but the girls were out of earshot. Beatrice backed away from her father with a nostalgic look in her eye.

"I think—"

"*Don't.*" Kitty cut her sister off and stepped in between her two older relatives. "Don't do this. I suppose she's sick until she's live on air, right? Beatrice has been away for too long, but I know what you've done with Glenn. She's just like you, it's too late for her. She's an *addict.*" Kitty spat on the ground between Hersey's feet. She turned, grabbed her sister by both of her shoulders, and began walking away.

"Wait!" Hersey's desperation intensified, and his daughters hesitated before turning around. "About the letter; how did you know I was coming to Mexico?" Hersey looked to Kitty as he asked this. To his surprise, it was Beatrice who cleared her throat.

"We saw the *boos*, they were all over TV." Beatrice said. "We've known you for a really long time, Hersey. You're not as unpredictable as you think."

❦1999❧

"Kitty—" Glenn gasped, excited with surprise that was cut off when her sister marched past without so much as a glance in her direction. Locked in on the bodies that stood—fake smiles and all—at the bottom of the staircase, Kitty didn't notice the hand-shaped bloodstain when she stepped on it during her bee-line towards the back of the room.

"*You!*" Kitty's accusation aimed through the wand of her boney fingertip. Her hair was tied into tight, brown braids to match the dirt that covered her overalls and boots. Kitty's finger shook as she pointed between the eyes that grew wide in defense of such scrutiny.

Brown nail polish gleamed against the light of the chandelier that hung over all of their heads. Kitty's voice was husky and abrasive, it carried so much weight that Elroy found himself clutching to Hersey's chest in anticipation of the attack.

Kitty didn't stop with just one startling word, though. Her pointed finger came mid-stride and she stormed onto the stairs. She ignored both her father, and the vaguely familiar old man that fell into his arms. She didn't stop until she shared a step with her oldest and guiltiest sister.

"Me?" Beatrice faded away from Kitty. She seemed to speak in ignorance, but Kitty leaned even closer when her sister drifted. Two beakish noses hovered only about an inch away from each other, they hung in suspended animation, nearly eskimo kissing as they drifted like lances extended for jousting. Finally, Beatrice straightened up, realization washed over her face and she took a step back from the intensity of Kitty's aggressive greeting.

By now, both Hersey and Elroy had retreated down the stairs to join Glenn. They stood and they stared from their perch next to the mansion's front door. The sun peaked out from the clouds, it shined through the frontroom's stained-glass windows and washed the whole room with a reflection of soft purple light.

Kitty craned an arm to reach into the breast pocket of her coat, everybody flinched. She came out with a whipping motion, everybody held their breath. She brandished a flopping edition of *The Daily Dilemma,* and the rest of the room shared in a sigh of relief. "Care to explain?" Kitty spat venom with the words in her throat. To this, Beatrice smiled. She was glad to see a magazine instead of a gun, a knife, or a suspicious looking ballpoint pen. Though a secret agent gig would have been a good explanation for Kitty's recent absence from the family.

"What do you mean?" Play dumb, it was always better to keep Kitty in a docile mood. Kitty responded by tearing pages with violent flips, she ripped until she reached an old family photo that stretched across a two-page spread near the middle of the tabloid. Kitty turned the page over to face the rest of the family. Tilting her nose into the air, she began to read aloud.

"*James Gang: The Next Generation.* This reboot is set to introduce a new member of Hersey James's legendary family to the public!" Kitty faked enthusiasm, mocking a newscaster's tone as she read. "What happened to Glenn? Everyone's favorite toddler of the seventies has grown up and been replaced by her party-girl sister for the updated version of the show! Is something wrong in the life of Glenn James? Find out in our exclusive interview with upcoming showrunner and Producer extraordinaire Elroy Bartholomew."

Kitty's eyes narrowed into half-moons that locked in on Beatrice. Her arms went limp as they dropped to her thin waist, she allowed the magazine to slip through her fingers. "I know I'm not the party-girl they're talking about."

Beatrice shared a defeated look with her younger sister. The purple glow of the room had lit Beatrice's face into a vibrancy that mixed her pale skin into pink. Kitty sank into her sister's eyes, it was as if she were swimming inside of them. Swimming, and searching for something very specific, something that only a sister could ever even think to look for. Kitty squinted, and judging by the look on her face, she was searching for something that had left a long time ago.

Glenn, frozen with her hand still grasping onto the crystal doorknob, broke the pain of this particular searching-silence with just one word. *"Beatrice?"*

Glenn stood closest to the purple window, the light cast against her white gown and burst into a beautiful, delicate stream of color. A white light shone with the sound of her breaking voice, it was as if the sun chose to glow in bright purple that day. It was light, but it had been tarnished by the tears that fell onto her gown's white lapel.

"Is it true?" Glenn asked with vocal chords that rattled as she spoke. Glenn's face entered a shadow as the light shifted outside. While the rest of her body was still lit up in a beam of angelic purple, Glenn's face could be seen in perfect clarity. Beatrice turned away from Glenn and back towards Kitty, it was easier to act tough in front of a braver face.

"It is." Beatrice hung her head and whispered the room into silence that strained as it tried to hear her hoarse words.

Kitty looked at Beatrice, Glenn looked towards her father, something stank. With simultaneous sighs, both girls turned towards their counterpart, and spoke in strict, polite syncopation. "Can I see you in my room, please?"

Hersey's face fell, Beatrice's lit up. Hersey's shoulders slunk towards the blood stained floor, Glenn knew him too well to alleviate his share of the blame in all this. Beatrice, on the other hand, let the weight fall from her clenching cheeks. Kitty seemed to be calming down, everybody was safe for now.

Beatrice had always been able to feel Kitty's spells coming on in advance. She would feel a pressure that ached through her temples, it pounded her brain in pulses that felt as if she had sunk deep into the depths of the ocean. The pressure would build until it turned into a scalding heat that dominated the feeling inside of Beatrice's ears.

Soon after the heat, like clockwork, Kitty would explode. Tears, broken vases, broken bones, nothing was off limits once the heat had risen into Beatrice's head. This time Beatrice had gotten lucky, though, she smiled as she followed her sister to the room that neither of them had seen in several months. Beatrice walked with a head that recovered from its ache without having to feel the heat.

The inside of Kitty's room matched the inside of just about every outdoor magazine that Beatrice had (accidentally) seen. Cutouts of skiers, snowboarders, hikers, mountain-climbers, scuba-divers, sky-divers, campers, fishers, photographers, and just about anybody else who had hugged a pine tree in the seventies. The images wrapped the entirety of Kitty's room in a wallpaper of escapism.

Kitty led her sister in through the door, she sat down on the bed and wrapped her legs up in the brown sheets that rippled like a rising tide around her sun-baked body. "Close the door?" Kitty requested, and with the arrival of her voice came a forced gentleness that cut into her words and hinted at something that boiled beneath the surface. Beatrice squirmed as she shut the door and took a seat next to her sister. The room was dark and suffocating, the wallpapering cutouts covered the room's windows and blocked most of the sun from shining in. The only light that came through was a dim, musty kind, twice filtered between the glue and the papers.

"You probably think I'm just *aching* with jealousy right now. Don't you?" Kitty crossed her legs beneath the bedspread as she spoke. Immediately and obviously, it became apparent that Beatrice was at a loss for words. So Kitty continued. "You probably think that I've been *jealous* this whole time. Haven't you?"

"I guess it never entered my mind." Beatrice's mouth hung open. It was as if she were sending a subliminal illustration about the emptiness of her words.

"Oh Beatrice." Kitty said. "You don't expect me to believe that, do you?" Another blank expression and more silent fidgeting, that was all Beatrice had to offer in response. "So all the solidarity we found in hatred, all the *James Gang* jokes that we made over the years, all the disdain for our father's obsession, for our sister's meritless stardom, everything we've said…"

Kitty paused for a moment that stretched into a thoughtful eternity. "I just can't believe you're going to work with Hersey! I mean, after everything he did to us, after everything he did to ruin our relationship—you're just going to ignore all of that?" To this, Beatrice stood up and took a step backwards. Back towards the door, and back away from her sister's potential reach. Something had appeared inside of Kitty's eye, something that boiled in red heat and appeared from deep within. It boiled and spread to Beatrice's head. Kitty rose too.

"What're you doing?" Beatrice stammered as she backed away. Reaching with a blind hand, she found the door behind her.

"Why'd you get up?" Kitty answered her sister's question with one of her own. "Surely you don't think I'm so feeble anymore, do you?" Kitty approached her sister with palms up as a kind of peace offering.

"Feeble, never." Beatrice said, slowing her retreat as she inched closer to the door. "Feeble-minded, weak-willed, too scared to admit— even to yourself—what it is that you truly want." Fear shook Beatrice's voice as she spoke. Something had possessed her to speak her mind, but her bravery was only as deep as her voice box.

"And what might that be?" Kitty's menacing march paused. Momentarily. Something new had replaced the blind rage that stoked the fire inside Kitty's eye. Where confusion replaced rage in Kitty's head, bravery replaced fear in Beatrice's. Momentarily.

"That would be fame, Kitty." Beatrice straightened up. She closed her mouth back into a frown, and tilted her head back up towards the sky. "That would be the human condition, my dear."

"No, not for me. You sound like your father." Kitty turned her head.

"Take that back!" Beatrice took a step forward and screamed through her eyes as she spoke. "It's the desire of anyone with a pulse who is smart enough to recognize that it will stop one day. Fame, something to leave behind for the aliens to find when they come down from the sky in a million years. Long after we're all dead, when the human race has been sucked into a black hole or something—somehow, somewhere, there'll be a rerun of *The James Gang* playing. That much, I can guarantee."

Beatrice smiled in a kind of sad way. She was calming down. "The world's going to remember versions of us that we've never even met, Kitty. I've been turned into a character that was perpetuated by my father. Surely you can't blame me for taking that back from him."

Kitty sat back down on the bed. Once again, Beatrice had succeeded in dousing her sister's flame. Beatrice turned towards the wall and ran her hand along a magazine cutout that depicted a lion in the heat of the morning on the Kenyan savannah. The lion's hackles were all the way up, and it approached a zebra with a leg that had already been crushed into what looked like ground hamburger meat. The approach was slow, it was as if the lion wanted to bask in every moment of this victorious hunt. He breathed deep, and smiled the way only a lion can smile.

Beatrice knew that the lion was acting on instinct. It was hungry, and acting as all hungry creatures must. Still, she couldn't help but to think of this image as an act of victory over the prey. The lion—rejoicing in its victory lap—wanted the zebra to know exactly who it was before it sank its teeth in for the fatal blow.

"And don't worry about Henry, my dear." Beatrice locked eyes with the lion in the picture. Behind her, Kitty's face glazed with solemnity. "He may have replaced you in the show, but there's *no* replacing the *real deal*." Beatrice smiled, still staring at the lion. Oblivious, in her own world of deep study, barely even able to register the sound of her own voice as it left her mouth. Oblivious, in her own world of deep study, unaware of the brown-clothed girl that stormed out and slammed the door behind her.

Hersey James appeared to age a decade for each step that he took, he was a dead man walking by the time he made it all the way up the stairs to Glenn's room. His cheeks had hollowed into pits that shadowed and appeared as dark circles on either side of his face. Though each step he took was a miracle in the practice of standing upright, Hersey James had broken his own heart.

Glenn held the door for the hobbling, shrinking man, with a polite smile. One that didn't spread across her entire face like usual. This smile was damned in, never daring to leak away from the confines of her grass thin lips. She released the door to let it close behind her and it slammed all on its own, Hersey flinched at the sound of such an aggressive gesture. However unintended it may have been, he shriveled. A fetus, he crumpled as he had at the beginning of his life, identical to his posture of an end. Glenn opened her mouth, but the room rang with the sound of a voice that wasn't her's. Evading time for a moment, Hersey had beaten her to the punch.

"I'm sorry! Oh Glenn—" Hersey blubbered. "How could you ever forgive me? I've been such a terrible father to you. You probably want to cast me out, you probably want to abandon me as your sisters have! Lord knows I've given you good reason—"

"Enough!" Glenn's voice erupted into sound. She glared at her father, she sucked her lips in-between her teeth and rolled her fingers up into fists that drained her skin of color. Sheclenched those in close to her hips.

"Glenn, you have to believe me. I don't even know how that article got published! I wasn't even aware of the show until Beatrice showed up this morning. It was her, her and that corporate minion of tabloid evil that she's attached to her side!" Hersey spat as he spoke, his weight shifted back and forth from one navy blue boat shoe to the other. Beads of cold sweat began to form underneath the brim of his beret.

"Is that why Beatrice came back, to talk you into erasing me?" Glenn twirled her fingers into loops around each other, tightroping the line between confusion and spite.

"Erasing you?"

"Isn't that what you'd call it?"

"My dear, I would never erase you!"

"Then the article's lying?"

"Well…" Hersey strained his neck to the side. His veins turned visible through a thin coat of skin, they were blue and spread like a virus. A family portrait hung on the wall above Glenn's canary colored bed, it caught Hersey's attention as he stirred. All of a sudden, Hersey stopped speaking and dropped his knees onto the mattress. He crawled over the sheets to get a closer look of the photo, and the seven smiling faces that stood, arm-in-arm, inside of it. "Do you remember this?" Hersey asked. Glenn stood in the middle of the picture; Henry, Gretchen and Hersey on one side, Beatrice and Kitty on the other.

"Of course I do." Glenn said, her eyes drifted towards the ground as to avoid the object of her father's gaze. She knew exactly what he was talking about. "It was my first day on set in New York. You were the world's great American father-figure, and I was their sweetheart. I really can understand why you would want all that to come back, dad. I really can." Glenn allowed her gaze to drift up towards the picture on the wall. She leaned onto the bed next to her father, she brushed his shoulder with a strand of canary-colored hair that fell and camouflaged against the bedspread.

"Don't they look happy?"

"Which ones?"

"Your sisters—Beatrice and Kitty, I mean." Hersey turned back towards Glenn with a toothless grin that made his eyes squint and disappear within the sea of lines on his face. "I don't think I've seen them like that ever since. They were children then. From the looks of it, we all were."

Glenn began to speak, but she cut herself off. She paused to analyze her words before letting them go. "They both cried themselves to sleep that night." Glenn's mouth hung open, she poked her chin forward and studied the changes in her father's face. And his face did change. "I don't remember all that much about this night." Glenn motioned back towards the photo. "But I'll never forget their crying."

"*Sh*—Surely your young memory must be blowing things out of proportion!" Hersey laughed and lifted himself back off of the bed. "I mean, who could cry after spending all day on the set of a TV show? Why, that would be a dream for anyone. Wouldn't it?" Hersey's smile faded, Glenn felt the weight of his gaze shift as he refocused his attention onto her.

Glenn was soon to follow her father's suit of physical motion. Though she glided as she moved while her father turned the rusted gears that were his joints, Glenn too got up from the bed. She turned in cautious steps, ones that shuffled as she turned to look her father in the eyes.

"Maybe it took them a couple of hours."

"A couple of hours, for what?" Hersey interrupted his daughter, he raised his voice in preemptive defensiveness.

"Maybe it took them a couple of hours before they realized that they were posing for pictures with their clones." Glenn snapped. Her words came out in knives that sliced her father with the precision of her tongue. It was as if they were back in the foyer, reciting old lines and faking tension until the scene ended and they wound up in the laughing embrace of nostalgia. This time, Glenn's lips wobbled as she stared her father in the eyes. She had never been *that* good of an actor. This time, there was no part to play.

"My dear, are you alright?" Hersey leaned in when he noticed the tears that welled in his daughter's eyes. Her trembling lips shook and she raised her eyebrows into a wrinkle-less kind of frown. Only breathing through her nose, she exhaled and it sounded like choppy blows on a whistle. Hersey reached out to put a hand on Glenn's shoulder, but she pulled away from his grasp. Facing the bed, with only a back to face her father, she tried to laugh when she spoke.

"*Wh*—Why did you pit me against them? You turned me into a character on TV. You turned me into a character—and now you're ripping it away!" Hesitantly, Hersey backed away as he listened to the back of his daughter's head. "I'm not Glenn James anymore, in a sense. I'm not Glenn, Beatrice is Glenn."

"I suppose you want to be left alone, then." Hersey said. "I wish you would forgive me, but I can see that you need some alone time." Hersey's hand wobbled right along with the beat of his daughter's lips. "I'm a patient man, you can never say I wasn't patient, so take all the time you need." He backed out of the room.

To Hersey, the world outside had become a screaming, stomping, spitting, red-faced mess that was just waiting to welcome him in with a punch in the face and a shove into the concrete. As he exited Glenn's room in disgrace, it became clear to Hersey that he had let too much of the outside world into the four-walled sanctuary that was the *James Gang* mansion.

Something whistled near the kitchen. The sharp screech could only have been coming from the tea kettle. The screech drowned underlying sounds out the way a police car's siren might cover the noise of a city's unrest as it races through the streets. Hersey bristled at the thought that his precious home could conjure such a barbaric comparison.

Hersey marched towards the backyard with the mysterious disturbances on the front of his mind, and thoughts of Glenn to occupy the back. He pitied the girl, he pitied her so much that he almost even thought about rejecting the reboot. Almost. His boat shoes squeaked against the red marble staircase with a sound that reminded Hersey of nails on a chalkboard. He sped up, gradually nearing the noise that became apparent beneath the squeak of the kettle. The man of the house, he strode until, all of a sudden, a thunderous *squeal* and *crash* froze his feet to the bottom step.

The whistling sound of the tea kettle had ceased and been replaced by voices. It was deep, it was Kitty, uh-oh.

Wincing when he walked, Hersey feared what he may see as he turned the corner towards the backyard. He leaned outside for a moment before making his full presence known.

Water splashed into the air and bounced off Hersey's raincoat when he brought the rest of his body outside. Two bodies flailed in front of him, splashing and struggling in the pool while the shards of the Victorian tea kettle lay in tatters by the edge of the water. Kitty had Elroy by the shoulders. An evil look had ignited the heat in her face, and her eyes glazed over as if a possession had occurred. She shoved Elroy into the water, submerging his gasping breath while she jumped on top of him. "Old man always needs his controversy." Kitty muttered, and just as she pulled Elroy up, she splashed him in again.

Hersey dove in. Newly a man of action, he sprang from his old man joints and caught a moment of youth as he splashed into the pool beside the warring two. With one hand on the scruff of Kitty's neck, the old man became a father again. He yanked and pulled, dragging his daughter until she was out of the water and wading in the pool of broken porcelain that scattered the water's edge. Kitty glanced at the mess, and Hersey knew exactly what had happened.

"You didn't." Hersey said.

"She smashed it!" Elroy chimed Holding his gaze at Kitty, he shook his head in slow, parental disappointment, and caught his breath on his way out of the pool.

The gray of Kitty's face had heated into a deep red. Her chest rose and fell in heaves that alluded either to a spell of screaming, or of violent sickness. She stared at her father as if Elroy had ceased to exist, she locked in on him with gritted teeth and clenched fists. Hersey's face heated too, it turned red to match his daughter's, and the two James's seethed in momentary silence.

This redness was a preemptive strike. "Don't start with me." Another preemptive strike, a classic tool within Kitty's arsenal of weaponry. "Not with me. *Never*, with me." Kitty's eyes rounded into a bloodshot scowl. She had inherited her father's stinging peepers, and tears never helped the irritation.

"First of all, hello." Hersey said. He crossed his arms and tried to condense the totality of his rage into one passive-aggressive statement. His voice sounded as if it were begging for something. "It's been far too long, my darling."

"I wonder why!" Kitty threw her hands up to the sky. She rolled her eyes to the end of their straining span.

"You know, sometimes I really do wonder that very same thing!" Hersey shook his head, he mocked his daughter's sarcasm with an over the top sense of sincerity. "Was I ever so poor to you? I mean, you and that sister of yours—" Hersey swallowed hard. "Some people would've killed for a father like me. For a mansion to grow up in, for open doors to welcome them whenever they dain to make an appearance. *Y*—You and that ungrateful, spiteful, older sister of yours—" Hersey paused for a breath. Apparently his old age had seized the ability to talk and breathe at the same time.

Hersey's eyes narrowed into red slivers of stinging, resentful passion. He clutched at the bottom of his coat with two ever-needy hands. His gaze darted between the eyes of his daughter and the priceless tea kettle that lay in pieces on the ground between the two of them. Tea kettle, to Kitty, to tea kettle, back to Kitty. "You're weak." Hersey spat and settled his gaze onto his daughter. "Both of you; born to play the victim."

That seemed to shut her up. Even if it was only for a moment, the peace of the *James Gang* mansion had returned to its rightful state of even-keeled hibernation. Kitty had stopped breathing. There were words on her lips, but they hid behind a closed mouth for almost an entire minute before finally, they managed to pry themselves free.

"And what about Glenn?" Kitty spoke slow, almost slurring as she asked. "Does she deserve this?" The magazine had reappeared, it was soggy in Kitty's hand and she smiled a sympathetic smile, one that had no specific target. The magazine—still open to the article that began with *James Gang: The Next Generation*—stared back at Hersey as if it were daring him to plead for forgiveness.

"I take no responsibility for that." Hersey turned his head away from the pages.

"Oh, so it's wrong then!" Kitty raised her voice, sarcastic in her glee. "So Glenn isn't being replaced, so this show isn't coming back to tear my life to shreds like it did the first time around? So we're all free to live our lives in avoidance of *your* ego, so you've made peace with your fade into obscurity?" Hersey shot a glance down towards Elroy. Bug-eyed and clinging onto what remained of his pride, he received a lifeline.

"We got an exclusive story!" Elroy piped up, more than willing to forgive an assault for the sake of his next big show. "They needed content at the magazine, and we had a story to tell. Surely there's no crime in seizing an opportunity!" Elroy smiled, he nodded his head and reached out to both sides of his withering body. He extended one hand to each warring party, smiling as if he were staging some historic peace treaty between rival countries. "And besides, if anyone's life was ruined back then, it was Beatrice. And now she's leading the charge!" Elroy winked at Hersey. Kitty—believe it or not—pulled away.

"Kitty?" A voice called from the staircase. It wasn't deep. It was Beatrice.

She *clomped* with confused feet that *clacked* against the marble staircase. Her voice carried and swirled around the patio. It silenced everything that it touched with its sound. "Kitty, where'd you go? I wasn't done talking to you." The entirety of the yard held painfully still, even Elroy didn't seem especially keen on Beatrice at that moment. The birds held their songs in the trees, even the wind quieted its rustling in the bushes. "Kitty!" Beatrice *clomped* into the backyard. Even in a mansion that sprawled like this one, it's a tall task to hide forever. "Why'd you walk out on me?"

"Maybe I'd had enough of the speeches for one night." Kitty scratched at the dirt on her overalls.

"Oh, don't be so dramatic!" Beatrice waved her cigarette carrying hand in a *wax off* sort of motion. "You need me to give you these speeches, darling."

"Why's that?" Kitty sneered.

"Because without me and all my wisdom. My dear, you'd be out to sea without a sail!" Beatrice laughed. Her eyes drifted towards Elroy, then he laughed, and then they drifted towards Hersey, and he laughed too. It was all very funny if you happened to have a vested interest in the happiness of the all-powerful Beatrice James. "I'm worried about our Glenn." Beatrice took a step back and projected her voice to address the entire group. Like a

Shakespearean actor who plays to the seats in the back row of their cavernous theater, she straightened her back and bellowed without screaming.

"What! Why?" Hersey lunged forward with pure, reactive adrenaline. He was too old to get anywhere too fast, but the reflex was charming in its way.

"Why do you think?" Beatrice spoke through a pair of lips that only opened near the cigarette-free portion of her mouth. "She's been crying like a whale ever since you left her room, Hersey. What'd you say to her in there?"

"Oh don't you blame this on me!" Hersey yelled and bent his knees as if he were preparing for a second lunge. "You were the one that came in here and shook everything up. You were the one that ran with that story before anyone agreed to it!" Hersey—exhausted by his own excitement—collapsed his hands to his knees and paused for a calming breath. "I was trying to explain myself to her. She got very upset." Hersey panted. "You took her from me, *she*—" He gasped. "*She was*—"

"Spit it out for Christ's sake!"

"She was the last one who loved me!"

Elroy placed a hand on Hersey's arching back. Beatrice and Kitty milled in tandem, grumblings bubbled up from deep inside their throats, and their hands clasped behind their backs. Hersey's spine trembled, and massaging the palm of Elroy's hand in sporadic ripples that lurched down from Hersey's throat. "That wasn't a professional sort of cry." Beatrice theorized with a level head. "No, No, I've had my fair share of professional cries. They wail and they moan, they cry in broad strokes. They don't shudder, Glenn was definitely shuddering."

"It was a cry for *family!*" Hersey blubbered from his standing take on the fetal position.

"Nope." Kitty said.

"Glenn may be thick, but she isn't thick enough to let a betrayal come as that much of a surprise. Not from us, not from *you.*" Beatrice explained, somehow remaining calm while managing to be extremely accusatory.

"You mean from *you?*" Hersey's voice strained.

"Regardless, we *must* get to the bottom of whatever seems to be troubling our little girl!" Beatrice ignored her father's accusation. "I think I should try to talk to her, you all would just do more damage."

"*Me?*" Kitty asked. "What kind of damage have I done? I'm not the one who lost my knife in her back!"

"Oh, shut up!" Beatrice and Hersey shouted in unison, though Beatrice continued her defense without the help of her father. "This rescue mission requires lots of care." Beatrice spoke slowly, she spoke as if she were trying to illustrate her point to a toddler. "And care, my dear, has never been your strong suit." Beatrice smiled, delighted with her attempt at softening the blow. Hersey straightened his back and wiped the tears from his eyes as he did so.

"It should be Beatrice." Hersey—recovering from his mourning period—put on a brave face to look at Kitty. "We wouldn't want anything shattering while you're up there." He sneered. "Elroy, come with me to my office. We shouldn't let this little distraction get in the way of our great revival." Elroy checked Beatrice for a nod of approval. He received it, and followed Hersey out of the kitchen. Beatrice smirked at Elroy before walking back up the stairs.

"Glenn?" Beatrice tapped on the door to her sister's room. "Glenn, may I come in?" More tapping, unanswered. More calling, unanswered. Soon calling turned to begging,

begging turned to yelling, tapping turned to knocking, and knocking turned into banging. "Let me in you hermit! What'll you do for water? I swear to God if you don't open this door I'm going to come back with a sledgehammer!" Beatrice yelled until her face turned pink and her hand started to throb against the hard teak of the door.

Beatrice was just beginning to notice a breakage in her voice when she felt a surprise poke against one of her knelt knees. The prick had slipped through the bottom of Glenn's door and brought Beatrice's attention to the floor; there, one yellow notecard stuck out from the door's crack and jammed a corner against Beatrice's knee. She picked it up and read.

"Dearest Beatrice. You may think I despise you, and while part of me hopes to find you in dire disarray about this whole scenario, I highly doubt that is the case. Instead, I imagine you as being deep in the throws of denial. No doubt, you think that I would've done the same to you if I were in your place. And while I can't say I wouldn't, I can say that I don't particularly want to defend myself about that right now. I hope you understand and will promptly leave me to unwind in the comfort of my own room. If you still consider yourself a sister, even after all that you have done to hurt me, you will respect that wish and grant me one more. Send for Henry Elliott first thing tomorrow morning. Don't ask questions, just do it.

P.S. Don't tell them what you know.
Yours forever, Glenn James."

Inside Glenn's room, a white cat rested and purred. It stretched out underneath her bed and batted at the sheets that overflowed and hung over its side. The purr was being drowned out by Nico, who was singing "Chelsea Girls" from the inside of Glenn's record player. Nico—also the name of the cat—had no idea that she was listening to her namesake over the speakers.

Glenn's nose poked the mirror that stood, vertical, by the foot of her bed. Her breath fogged the image of her chin with each exhale and cleared up as each inhalation recaptured that moisture.

Glenn met her own eyes in reflection, tears dripped down her cheeks and mixed with the excess of black hair dye that escaped from her scalp. Gloved fingers ran through her hair, more dripping and more tears. Glenn's eyes stung, they turned red and resembled those of her father. She saw him in the eyes in the mirror, so she wept some more.

By now, Beatrice had almost certainly left. Glenn wondered if she would send for Henry as she had requested in her note. Her scalp began to throb and her once golden head began to ooze into the desired shade of black.

Behind Glenn, beyond Nico's purrs and the canary-colored sheets, each of the picture frames that lined Glenn's bed had been turned around to face the wall.

Glenn trembled as she ran one last glove through her hair, what was once angelic had become coarse and rigid. What was once the hair that she recognized from her youth, the blonde locks that shined in reruns of *The James Gang*, had changed.

Black, the black in her hair beckoned a certain kind of maturity. Glenn looked at herself with the black hair that still seemed like a wig to her, and believed in her own mortality for the first time in her life. She clamped her eyes shut as a final run of black dye streamed past the corner of her eye and onto her nose. Even her tears had lost their color.

On her way to meet Hersey and Elroy in the office, Beatrice was surprised to find Kitty in the kitchen. She sat there, head down at the head of the teak kitchen table. She bounced her knee and shot a restless glance when she heard the *clack* of Beatrice's high-heeled step.

"How is she?" Kitty asked.

"She'll be okay." Beatrice responded without breaking her stride. She had completed her descent from one staircase and was trying to make it to the other without catching herself in this web of sisterly conversation. "Lot's of moody music going on up there, I suppose she's just having a moment."

"Ah, I'd trust you to know a thing or two about that!" Kitty smiled, fully aware that her words had the power to stop her sister in her tracks. Kitty dodged a glare from Beatrice by shooting her eyes back down to the table, but the *clomp* of Beatrice's feet grew closer. A chair slid against the marble and practically screamed for Kitty to look up. And there Beatrice sat, knee-to-knee with her sister, across the corner of the kitchen table.

"You know—" Beatrice started. "Hersey and Elroy are probably signing that contract in blood right now. Then it won't matter how much you scream, or how much Glenn cries. I know *just* how persuasive he can be." Beatrice looked through her eyebrows, and a toothless smile peeled onto her lips in a satisfaction that deepened with each moment that passed in silence. "And besides, I know something that'll just about guarantee all of this."

"Well—" Kitty leaned back and took a couple deep breaths before she continued. "Maybe it won't be so bad."

"It won't?"

"I mean, how could it be worse than last time, right? Glenn will replace you as an outcast and I'll be the same as I ever was." Kitty's eyes grew heavy as she spoke, it was as if her own words were threatening to bore her to sleep. "Sure, it'll be hard. I mean, it won't be easy to see you get so close to Henry every day at work, but—"

"Oh my God, I have something to show you!" Beatrice, all of a sudden, was very interested in conversing with her sister. The Audrey Hepburn eyes grew wide and her arms extended across the table to clutch Kitty by the wrists. Kitty pulled back, but Beatrice wouldn't let go. Both wrists had been clamped by the vice grip of a woman with a secret.

"What is it?" Kitty asked, still cautious but losing the will to fight against her sister's surprising strength.

Beatrice reached down towards the note in her pocket. "It's about Henry *and*—" Beatrice began, but cries erupted from Glenn's room and stole the quiet from the mansion. The sound took Kitty's attention with it. These were sputtering, rippling, unbusinesslike cries. They detached themselves from the music of Glenn's room and deafened everything on their way down to the kitchen.

"You don't want her to get better!" Kitty sneered in disgust.

Beatrice began to defend herself, but Kitty's attention had fully turned to the top of the staircase. There, Glenn's door hung ajar for the first time in hours. Nico's voice had stopped, replaced by the lurching cries of the girl that hid inside. Kitty locked her attention onto the small crack in the door. With newfound strength, she pried herself from Beatrice's grip and tip-toed towards the staircase.

No action in the doorframe, the crack let out a small beam of light from the inside of Glenn's room. It always shined with the softest light. Kitty stared at the beam as she climbed the staircase with an abundance of caution. She scanned the gap for shadows, anything that hinted at movement. She continued her creep until a black figure illuminated itself against the backdrop of the light.

Kitty froze, her feet stuck to the top stair of the staircase. She would have reached out to the doorknob, but her arms had glued themselves to her side. The sobbing quieted, and Kitty quieted her breath in return. For a moment, she felt as if her sister were mirroring her from the other side of the door.

The shadow grew until it stretched through the door's gap and into the mansion's second story landing. The white cat, Nico, bounded out the door. Her glance darted around the room, only focusing on Kitty for a moment or two before bouncing to another object. Anything, one of equal meaning to the eyes of a cat.

Creak. Kitty's cat-induced trance was cut off by the sound of a door that drifted and clicked to a close. The music resumed, and Kitty found that she could only move her feet backwards. Back down the stairs from where she came. "You love having Glenn out of your way, you've become the coldest of all Ice-Queens. What was it that you had to show me?" Kitty spoke with impatient expectation as she returned to the kitchen. Beatrice hadn't moved.

"You care for her too much, you know." Beatrice ducked her head as if she were looking at Kitty through the tops of sunglasses that she wasn't wearing. "It's your fatal flaw. She's too far gone, remember? It *will* be the death of you."

"You speak like someone with a plan." Kitty said as she sat down, smiling. "Surely you couldn't be so certain unless you were planning to do the deed yourself!" The sisters shared a bated laugh. As outlandish as this kind of violence would have been for any family, both Kitty and Beatrice were conscious in tempering their laughter.

Beatrice leaned back, tilting her chair and flicking her sunglasses on to cover her eyes. One hand glided in and out of a green pocket, it emerged with two cigarettes and a lighter in between her forefinger and her thumb.

"Smoke?" Beatrice asked, flipping her hand around to expose the cigarette's filter to her sister.

"Of course." Kitty received the gift and a light to accompany it. She kicked her own seat back onto its hind legs. She mirrored her sister. "Some things never change." Kitty smiled, and Beatrice studied the smoke as it passed through her lips.

"You know…" She exhaled. "I hear that Henry Elliott's canceling his New Year's Eve party this year."

"We hate it there." Kitty spoke in a stern, deep voice. More of a command than a statement, really.

"No, *you* hate it there." Beatrice took another drag, letting her gaze wander as she did it. Eventually, she landed on the closed door that was still erupting with the sound of Glenn's moody blues. "I was rather looking forward to it this year." Beatrice smiled, Kitty laughed. "What?"

"I know you far too well to keep a straight face when you say something like that!" Kitty rolled her eyes.

"What's that supposed to mean?" Beatrice straightened her back and ashed her cigarette. She conjured her best, most sobering face, and refocused on her sister's gaze.

"I mean that things don't change so much!" Kitty smiled and allowed her cigarette to burn down between her fingers. "I know you, I knew you before you turned into Cruella Deville or whoever it is that you're pretending to be." Kitty leaned forward, she placed both of her elbows on the table in front of her. Once again, she mirrored Beatrice to a tee. "It's just like the cigarettes." Kitty exhaled and watched the smoke as it floated. "Some of these things are just facts of our lives." She went back in for a long, scholastic, drag from the cigarette that had almost burnt to an end by now. "Beatrice, my sister, we were *never* born to win." Kitty blew her smoke across the table and watched as it seeped behind Beatrice's bug-eyed sunglasses.

"You're just mad because you're *in love* with him."

"Who?"

"Who?" Beatrice mocked in delight. "You know exactly who I'm talking about."

"Shut your mouth." Kitty said with darting glances and a whispering voice. "You have no idea what you're saying right now—"

"Oh, spare me the theatrics! Like you said, we know each other. That boy's been through all of us. It's quite sad, really. I mean, when you think about the hold that he's got over this family." Beatrice said. "I know you trash him for rejecting you over, and over, and over, again." Her words drew out long, she delighted in the pain that each coming 'over' elicited on Kitty's face. "But I know you, and I can see in your face that you're just *desperate* for him to love you back."

"Is that what you wanted to tell me, then?" Kitty asked. "That the lowlight of my year has been canceled? Because if so, I really should be thanking you."

"Don't thank me quite yet." Beatrice folded her hands in front of her face, speaking through a mouth covered by fingers. She smirked, and it became obvious to Kitty that the secret was still intact.

Inside Glenn's room, only one Nico remained. Returning to its spin on Glenn's record player, her voice—singing "Eulogy To Lenny Bruce" by now—was undercut by the sporadic *snip* that came from the bed. There Glenn stood, sleek and oilish, the nature of her beauty had shifted. Drippings of left-over dye had stained her face with black streaks, and she was jerking to and from the top of her bed.

A new *snip* came with each new dive toward her bed's canary colored sheets. Her clothes lay on top of those sheets; white gown, purple flower-print tee shirt, pink sweater, white skirt, baby blue dress, white dress, yellow dress, purple dress, it didn't matter. She attacked, pressing a single blade of the scissors against the pad of her thumb, she used it and tore across the chest of her whitest gown. Her father loved that gown.

She moaned through lips that simply couldn't conceal themselves any longer, tears beaded and fell onto the clothes that she sliced. She sliced through the stomach of her red velvet prom dress, she sliced through the stomach of her pink premiere dress, she sliced through the stomach of her first modeling top, she sliced through the stomach of her old *James Gang* pajama shirt. Nico stopped singing when the needle drifted into the center of the record.

Now halted by the entry of silence, Glenn lifted her head from its focus on the clothes. Once lifted, she met her own gaze again, she had turned into something new within the confines of her room. Naked and damp with dye, Glenn shuttered and shut her eyes before tilting her gaze away from the mirror. She wept, "*Why?*"

The sound of this particular cry echoed throughout the *James Gang* mansion. It rattled the portrait of Scruffy James that sat noble in its frame on the wall in the foyer, it shook the purple stained glass until it loosened on the wall that surrounded the front door; it fell on four pairs of utterly deaf ears.

Now, these deaf ears were deaf because they were pointing in the wrong direction, locked in on the sound of the office door and the triumph that spewed from Hersey's office. Elroy—with hands extended towards God—was the first to emerge, and Hersey—with a light in his cheeks that hadn't been seen since the seventies—followed close behind. "Don't even tell me." Kitty locked eyes with her father.

"Welcome to a new era of the *James Gang's* legacy!" Elroy ignored Kitty's comment. He extended his hands out wide, beaming with a wrinkled kind of pride as he marched over to wrap Beatrice in a skeletal embrace. Kitty buried her head into hands that rested on the kitchen table, Beatrice hugged her father after hugging Elroy.

"I almost forgot what that felt like coming from you!" Hersey beamed.

"Don't push it."

In the background of such a joyous scene, with a birds-eye-view of the celebration, a trepidatious foot stepped out the door of her second story bedroom. There, Glenn James stepped onto the landing. "What's going on?" She sniffled her words to a room that fell silent. She forced a smile, though it was hazy behind the black cloud that wafted around her head.

"Glenn!" Hersey called, sounding as if he expected someone else to emerge from behind the new woman he saw. "My darling, what happened?"

"Nothing." Glenn said. She walked down the stairs and pivoted to face Beatrice. "I changed my mind, dear sister. I want to see him *now*."

"*Wh*—" Beatrice blushed and tried to speak, though the sound she made was more like a heavy exhale than anything that resembled tangible language. She looked at Kitty, trying to study the face that raised from the table without being noticed herself. "Well I don't think that's quite possible at such a late hour of the night." Beatrice turned her focus back around towards Glenn, whose gaze glazed over the tops of her eyes as if she hadn't slept in weeks. Glenn shuttered, she had always seemed so warm in her former, blonder state. Now she shivered in a chill that only she could feel.

"He will understand. Send for him." Glenn said. *"Do it now!"* Just then, her robotic speaking voice erupted into a scream. Everybody jumped and the party ended as suddenly as it had begun.

Beatrice, so close to her younger sister that she could feel the spit as it flew from her lip, jumped back further than the rest. With ghosts in her face—ghosts from a life of inferiority to the almighty Glenn James, ghosts that Beatrice thought she had vanquished in light of recent events—Beatrice whimpered "Of course." and she turned to sprint out the front door. Glenn stood in silence, a glaze had invaded her eyes and left the rest of her family, plus Elroy, to stare into a milky sheen.

"Glenn—" Kitty was the only one brave enough to speak. Though she spoke as if she were afraid to ask her question. "What did you just make her do?" Kitty spoke as slowly and as clearly as she could. The rest of the *James Gang* mansion fell silent apart from the *purr* of the cat that rubbed her face against the edge of Glenn's door. One last innocent soul in a mansion plagued by blemishes. Kitty repeated her question. "Why did you make Beatrice leave?" Slowly, again. "Where is she going?"

"Beatrice and I have a secret." Glenn said, watching the front door instead of looking her sister in the eye. "You'll find out soon enough." She spoke with a sigh that propelled her head towards the ground. Defeated by an enemy that was impossible to diagnose, Glenn turned and moped back up the red marble staircase that led to the door of her bedroom. Nico greeted her in silence, and Glenn followed her furry friend back through the door.

It was a short drive to Henry's apartment. Beatrice had made this quick trip countless times in the early nineties, and again every New Year's Eve whether she wanted to or not. While Beatrice wasn't used to seeing the outside of Henry's high rise without a layer of snow surrounding it, she was familiar with the flashing lights that lined the top floor of the locally famous Rimbaud Building. Henry was having a party.

Beatrice's head clouded as she parked, her ears rang with the frantic pitch of thought and she entered the building in a daze. Did she wish bad health onto Glenn as Kitty had suggested? Her most formidable roadblock on the trail to superstardom, at least Glenn was docile in her state of catatonic emotion. There was something of a demon in Beatrice, but there was also something holy, and that was exactly what possessed her when Glenn emerged to request the presence of her inconsistent lover of the past half-decade. It was something like empathy, it was some kind of sadness that her business would never approve of, it was a voice from Glenn in a mind that rang with regret from the sound of Hersey.

The top floor shook to the beat of the music that emanated from Room 919. Beatrice *clomped* across the hallway without any regard for the noise that she was making. If Henry's neighbors weren't already at the party, then it would have taken military-grade earplugs for them to fall asleep. Beatrice knocked on 919. She knocked a riff from a song, she couldn't remember its name, but Henry loved it. "Hey." A tall man answered the door, too tall and too strung out to be Henry, Beatrice frowned up at the giant.

"Is Henry Elliott around?" Beatrice had to lift onto her tip-toes in order to be heard over the sound of the party.

"Henry Elliott?" The tall man looked confused at first, he held his breath before breaking into the low rung of a Kitty-like laugh. He wouldn't stop, he just kept chuckling. "You mean the guy from *The James Gang*?" He took a sip from a red cup, then he chuckled some more. He doubled over in laughter and Beatrice took that as an opportunity to poke her head past him and into the apartment. "Henry!" She yelled, and the tall man reacted by flinching back up to a stand. He knocked his head against Beatrice's chin, and that sent him stumbling back in towards the middle of the room. He chuckled all the way as he went.

With the door clear, Beatrice entered the party. Blue and red lights flashed back and forth from a disco ball on the ceiling; people danced to pop songs, and an over-intricate drinking game had started in the kitchen; it was all very typical. "Henry?" Beatrice screeched her calls in a register that stretched to be heard over the sound of the music. She scoffed at the layman's drinks and entered the main room of the apartment. "Henry?"

"You looking for Henry Elliott?" Finally, a voice responded. He was slumped in Henry's loveseat, he was sinking in and shrinking within the frame of the furniture. He was a kind of inverse of the tall man that Beatrice had confronted at the door, Beatrice laughed to herself before responding.

"I am! Do you know where I can find him?" The shrinking man didn't seem too pleased to be doing this, but he raised his hand to point across the room.

"There." He said, and his arm collapsed back to rest on the loveseat. "Make sure you knock!" He laughed, and the entire population of the sitting area laughed along with him.

Beatrice did knock, she knocked in that same pattern that Henry used to like. It made her smile and it acted as a kind of identification device for Henry. He would recognize Beatrice immediately, just from the knock. She repeated the pattern, no answer. She repeated it two more times, nothing. So she barged in.

"*Whoa!*" Two bodies tumbled over the side of a couch when Beatrice opened the door. "Too much light, man!"

"Henry?" Beatrice recognized the voice, even if it was muffled from his war with his own furniture. Henry's head popped over the top of the cushion when he heard his name.

"Beatrice!" His face lit up, Beatrice's did not. He sprang to his feet to reveal a naked body. The room's blue light made him look paler than usual, and he had lost weight since she'd last seen him. Beatrice flinched when he hugged her. "What're you doing here?" He yelled his words. Straining to be heard over the permanent ring in his ears, he yelled even during the quietest parts of the music.

"C'mon Henry!" A flighty voice groaned from her hiding place behind the couch. "I'm not saving a thing for when you come back!" Right on cue, Henry's nose started dribbling with blood, he wiped it and laughed it off.

"New allergy medicine." Henry rubbed a t-shirt over his nose and waved the hiding voice off as he put it on. "Unless you're interested?" He shared a knowing look with Beatrice. His face lit up even more and he elbowed her in the ribs.

"Not today, darling." Beatrice smiled and twisted her body as if she were prying herself away from the couch. "I've actually got a bit of an emergency on my hands."

"Do tell." Henry's face sobered up, but his body bounced to the start of a new song. "Is it—"

"Yes." Beatrice nodded. "I'm afraid our girl's in bad shape." Beatrice made a point of scowling at the couch beyond Henry. "She won't leave her room, she won't speak to anybody; it's all quite pathetic." Beatrice turned and lit a cigarette, her match wouldn't light until her fifth try, her hands were shaking uncontrollably.

"She never called you pathetic, you know." Henry stopped bouncing. "In all the years, and all the times that she came running to me with emergencies like this back when you and I were dating... She never called you pathetic." Henry huffed, he sniffed the rest of the blood back into his nose and he started to walk out of the room. Beatrice followed.

"It's different!" Beatrice called after Henry as he led her out of the apartment. "She's totally lost control." Henry spun around just as he was about to enter the elevator.

"This *is* different. Glenn *is* different." Henry's lips and eyes shook in unison. His breath shuttered, he was serious. He was never this serious about anything.

"That wasn't my daughter." Hersey addressed the remaining kitchen-dwellers with a projection of certainty that stoked nods around the room. "That wasn't Glenn."

"I'm sure you're right." Elroy assured him, smiling in his face. The two old men aided each other as they sat down at the kitchen table. All three of them stared, Elroy and Hersey and Kitty, all waiting for someone else to speak. Soon Hersey's gaze fell to his hands, studying the lines in his palms until a crease sparked a memory, and a memory sparked a smile.

"Kitty, do you remember the story about my first season's coming home episode of *The James Gang*?"

"*Oh*—Please don't."

"Come on now, it's funny! Surely you don't want us to end this never-ending day in such sour moods. And Elroy's never heard it before!" Hersey smiled. He smiled at Elroy and got him to smile, he smiled at Kitty and she groaned. "Surely you don't want to ruin this day any more than you already have!"

"Fine!" Kitty's eyes grew wide with exasperation. "Remind me."

"If you insist!" Hersey was practically bouncing up and down in his seat by the time Kitty gave her confirmation. "So, Kitty was about thirteen years old during the first season of *The James Gang*. It was 'B.G.', before Glenn, and long before you met her." Hersey focused in on Elroy. "She was quite the firecracker back in those days, none of the dirty brown stuff that you've seen today. No, not back then,

I swear. Back then every little boy wanted her and every little girl wanted to be her. But she only had eyes for one."

"Oh my God." Kitty mumbled, blushing in bloody red and covering her face.

"I'm setting the scene!" Hersey objected before going on. "Anyways, this boy was Henry Elliott. I'm sure you're familiar with *his* work." Hersey gave Elroy a knowing chuckle. "Kitty was obsessed with Henry. So she forced her mother to take her to the set every single day during our lunch break—just so she could talk to the pimple-faced boy that played her on TV! She pined after him like nothing I'd ever seen, and on the day of our first season's final recording, she made her move."

"*Hmmph.*" Kitty sank into the kitchen table, infectious in her embarrassment.

"What did she do?" Elroy had begun bouncing right along with Hersey.

"I'm getting there, good man!" Hersey feigned exasperation, though he was secretly delighted to have gained such a captive audience. "She wanted to turn it into a grand gesture. So naturally, she waited until we were in front of our live audience to record. Then she plucked a few plastic flowers from our set and walked up to him. *Oh, Kitty*—what were your exact words again?"

"No."

"Oh c'mon, we've come this far! I'm an old man and the details have begun to escape me. But this is important." Hersey furrowed his thick eyebrow.

"I said, '*Hey Henry, wanna kiss me under the marquee at the Mabel's Movies tonight?*'" Kitty mocked her thirteen year old self by breaking her voice into a (slightly) higher pitch. She squeezed her shoulders up towards her ears.

Elroy couldn't contain himself, he spoke to avoid drooling all over the kitchen table in excitement.

"Oh yes, I'm remembering this one from *The Dilemma*! Remind me with your young mind, what did he say next?" Elroy vomited his words. Hersey smiled and picked the story back up to his own delight.

"He said, '*Beatrice?*'" Hersey threw his head back in silent laughter. "He said, '*Beatrice, I hardly know you!*'" Hersey doubled over, he leaned on the table as if his spine had failed in all his hysteria.

"Ouch." Elroy said, second hand blushing right along with Kitty.

"Ouch is right." Kitty echoed his sentiment.

"Ouch *is* right! But that's not even the worst part." Hersey delighted in each new word as if it were a sweet dessert, baked on one of his French travels from the show. "Kitty corrected him, you see. And once she did, he made this *terrible* face. He scrunched up into a million of the tiniest segments and *said*—oh Kitty, what'd he say again?"

"He said *'I know I've been accused of being a narcissist in the past, but wouldn't that be just like kissing myself?'* In that terrible British accent of his."

"Anyway." Hersey sent a side-eye to Kitty. "The whole set *erupted* in laughter. I mean, it was loud; camera crew, directors, boom operators, agents, reporters, and fans alike. They were all screaming their heads off. Isn't it funny? Isn't Henry just the picture of cleverness for coming up with that at thirteen?"

"Actually, I don't find it funny at all." Elroy milled in his seat. The corporate stooge had faded into the back of the closet of the old man who seemed to have so many hats. Hersey's smile faded.

"Well, Beatrice found it pretty funny." Kitty sighed. "She went on a date with him the very next week! I should've taken that as a sign, she's got betrayal in her blood."

"You mentioned reporters?"

"Oh yeah, they had a field day with the big rejection. I'm surprised you weren't on the scene to exploit it like usual." Hersey's smile returned with a nostalgic twinkle in his eye. "Newspapers, gossip magazines; you name it, the child-celebrity rejection was on the front cover of it. Taught you a thing or two about the media, didn't it?" Hersey straightened up, just enough to put a real fatherly tone into his question.

"I suppose so."

"I only wish that your sister paid better attention to your cautionary tale." Hersey grunted. "Lord knows, she could've used the advice around that time."

Just then, the sister in question opened the door. She gleamed with a put-on sense of pride as she glided back through the mansion's entryway. She glided like Glenn. The crystal doorknob presented no threat to her this time. "We have a visitor!" Beatrice sang her words through the foyer. Bravado, it can only be assumed, was deemed to be the best medicine to counteract the weak-will that she had exposed upon her sprint of an exit at Glenn's command.

"Well, speak of the devil." Hersey uttered his words as he lifted himself up from the kitchen table. He walked with stiff joints over to the foyer, he grew lighter on his feet as he walked towards the door. "Henry Elliott, back where he belongs!"

Kitty and Elroy watched from the kitchen table as Hersey hovered to the boy with the slick-back hair. They hugged, and it seemed for a moment that Hersey might cry. "How are you, my boy?" Hersey spoke wistfully before catching himself. "Oh, how rude of me. Come in, come in!" Hersey backed off and transferred his hug into a more dignified handshake. They walked into the kitchen to join Kitty and Elroy. "William would be proud to see us all together again."

"Henry Elliot…" Elroy got up and shook Henry's hand. "I'm sure you don't remember me, but I knew your father and I never forget a name. I am Elroy Bartholomew, and it's a great honor to be seeing you again."

"Hi Henry." Kitty waved, remaining seated, remaining red in the face. He waved back with a smile that was quick to fade. "So you're the mystery man that Glenn sent for?"

"I suppose so." Henry answered uncomfortably, scanning the corners of the room as if he expected Glenn to appear from a crevice or a closet.

"She's upstairs." Beatrice said, following the caravan into the kitchen from the foyer. Henry nodded and began to walk, but a hand stuck out and stopped him with a grasp onto his forearm. The hand was old and crossed with veins. Shaking, though surprising in the strength of its grip.

"Perhaps—" Hersey began, white-knuckling a tattoo of a masked cowboy that illustrated the underside of Henry's arm. "Perhaps you could shed some light on what all this is about? We are all very confused down here." Hersey's lip twitched into a self-conscious smile, and Henry's dilated pupils darted in every possible direction. Each except for that of Hersey's eyes, that is.

Henry smoldered like a shy model seeing his first camera's flash, he smoothed over the tremble in his voice when he spoke. "I think you'd better ask Glenn that one." Somehow maintaining respect with his movements, Henry scraped the old man's hand off of his arm. He rubbed the grasp-print that had turned white under the strength of Hersey's restraint.

"Go save her then." Hersey gave that same arm a gentle push. Biting his bottom lip and watching while Henry turned back towards the staircase, Hersey's eyes glazed into a long misty stare. "Go save our girl." His face began to glow in the kind of red that one would expect to find in the inside of a rare steak. Was he going to cry? Hersey James—being many things over the course of a jam-packed life—had never been a crier. Before long, in an act of valor that saved the entire kitchen from extreme discomfort, Henry disappeared through Glenn's door, and Hersey choked back his tears.

Light drained from the windows as time ran later into the night. The kitchen's radiance dimmed as it began to rely more heavily on the manufactured lighting of what few lamps stood in the corners of the room. Most of them were very warm in their shine, almost orange in their glow. They shone in a light that weighed heavy on the eyes, they shone in a light that had a tendency to slow the mind.

And minds did slow. The four waited while Henry stirred in Glenn's room, hopeful for him to emerge with lots of answers and Glenn by his side. But an hour passed, and the stirring rumbled on. It was consistent, the rumbling, with no sound of progress for better or worse.

Elroy's mind was the first to slow to a halt, he fell asleep right there with his hands propping his face over the kitchen table. He looked like a cherub longing dreamily for heaven. He stared beyond the lids of his eyes, and in looking at him one got the notion that the only thing tying him to his chair was his burden of earthly responsibility. *James Gang: The Next Generation*, there was earthly money to be made.

Soon, Kitty followed in Elroy's suit. Barely completing the stumble back to her room before passing out on top of her sheets. Beatrice held out for another ten minutes or so, but the power of the night proved to be too much for the most stubborn of the *James Gang* sisters. She fell asleep in her chair next to Elroy, craning down where he basked in the glow of his nearness to God. Hersey had barely sat down before he found himself alone in his wait.

With nothing to do but observe in his solitude, Hersey noticed that Henry had provided a bottle of wine to the counter on the other side of the kitchen. There's nothing more gentlemanly than providing an offering to accompany your visit, even in such a hurried call as the one that Henry got earlier in the night.

Henry mustn't have known that Hersey had climbed back on the wagon when Beatrice left for her third run through rehab. It had been quite some time since he'd seen the boy, and Henry had known the old man as more of a drinking buddy than a father-figure in that time.

Hersey smiled at the bottle, never ungrateful for a moment alone with what used to be a vice. The thought was in the right place. The wine was red, a 1970 Bordeaux Medoc, Hersey could tell just by looking at it. The red bottle illuminated in notes of lavender underneath the glow of the nearest lamp, and Hersey smiled once more, he projected confidence to the room that offered nothing in terms of reception. He shut his eyes to blind himself from the wine.

Hersey James reopened his field of vision to find himself sitting on the ground. His eyes were watering even more than usual, and Glenn's door towered only about an arm's length above his head. Hersey chuckled as he cried and reached forward. His fingers drifted along the grooved rectangles that framed Glenn's door into portions.

Hersey lined the bottom of the door with a delicate touch, not daring to move it even an inch. His mind raced with possibility about what could be happening on the other side. Gone was the crying, gone was the loud music. The room, from what Hersey could hear, had fallen into comparative silence. There was a constant pattering of mumbled discussion, there was even the occasional stir or squeak from the bed frame. Hersey listened intently and for a very long time, but nothing was large, there was nothing for Hersey to run with.

Any old man becomes an old man through an abundance of experience, and Hersey James was no exception. Time and time again, throughout his life, Hersey had run head-first into the very same problem that plagued him on this night. The only thing that could have trumped even this father's concern for his daughter, the only thing that could have trumped the commitment that his eyes had made to shedding their tears, was the familiar enemy of sleep. The next time Hersey James shut his eyes for a blink, it would last for hours.

"You're high." Inside Glenn's room, she whispered in shuttering tears that sent shame onto Henry. "You're high. I need you and you're loaded!" She cried.

"And you're hysterical!" Henry scorned in a quiet voice. "What's wrong with you, my dear?"

"What's wrong with me? You know what's wrong with me!" Glenn was struggling to keep her voice down, her lips quivered and she pushed away from Henry every time that he got close.

"Wrong? There's nothing for you to be ashamed of in any of this." Henry's tone was edging towards sorrow.

"Oh, it's a crime against the universe!" Glenn dumped herself face down into bed. That's how she slept that night. She stirred and rocked back and forth, but her face remained planted into her pillow. "It's a crime against a world of unconditional love. *Oh Henry*—We've *doomed* the world!"

The mansion was dewey in the morning, it was as if all the angst from the night before had solidified and evaporated over the course of the night. It left steam on the windows and a thin layer of mist to cover the marble floor that Hersey had slept on. Perhaps somebody had left a window open, the damp air cooled Hersey's eyes when they opened and the water made him think of his long-lost friend. William Elliott would have loved to wake up to a morning like this.

Hersey James peeled himself off of the floor of the second story landing with a sense for the nostalgic. William Elliott would have stayed up with him last night, a friend like that just doesn't leave another to sleep on the ground by himself. Hersey walked down the stairs to the kitchen.

Beatrice, Elroy, and Kitty were all already up. Fit with bright faces and tangled hair, they were making breakfast in the kitchen. Beatrice and Elroy took turns smiling at Hersey as he joined them by the stove. Beatrice offered him a mug and he sat next to Kitty, who was face deep into a plate of eggs and unresponsive to her father's attempts at exchanging pleasantries.

"Any word from the hermit?" Beatrice asked her father, under the illusion that he had come from Glenn's room and not his sleep on the floor.

"I'm afraid not." Hersey said. "Lots of stirring, still no word." The room let out a collective huff of frustration, the sound of which snapped Kitty back into the world that existed outside of her eggs.

"Out of all the people in the world…" She began. "Henry Elliott."

"Who, me?" A self-assured voice swallowed the room with the sound of his words. He smiled a kind of inward smile, and he trotted down the stairs. Henry Elliott had reemerged from the dungeon of the hermit. His slick-back hair had been sculpted into the shape of a spike at the center of his forehead, and his smile beamed with an impossible white. His eyes met the James's with a twitch in his stare and a tremble in his gaze. Everyone rose to their feet, eager to meet the one who seemed to be holding all the answers.

Nobody asked the question that was on their mind. Eight feet crowded Henry, they were moths gravitating towards light with open mouths and expectant ears. Henry knew the question, no words were needed. "I plead the fifth!" The boy closed his eyes and put one hand to his heart while holding the other one into the air, he swore on a pretend bible that had no place in the *James Gang* mansion.

"Oh, come on!" Kitty exclaimed, though nobody cared because a door opened, squeaked to its full extent, and clicked shut as she screamed.

"It's not my place to say." Henry shrugged, speaking like a line leading the room's attention to the second story landing, his gaze wandered with all the rest of them.

There, Glenn James stepped out of her bedroom, one bare foot at a time. Her black gown matched the dyed darkness of her hair. One rigid cut through the stomach of her dress was enough to expose a ghostly midriff that swayed from side-to-side as those timid feet crept down the stairs. Her toe-nails were still painted with the canary kind of yellow that matched the sheets on her bed, one last remaining whisper from the vibrance of her youth. Her eyes, like milky marbles that wobbled as she walked, watered and gleamed with white light as she spoke.

"He's right." Glenn forced a smile, it was the same shape as it always had been, but the whole thing reeked of the darkness that reflected from her new hair onto those smiling teeth. "Goodmorning, everybody!" A wash of red embarrassment drifted over her face and she stopped on the lowest step.

"Well?" Kitty rolled her eyes at the sight of that smile. That smile might as well have been a commercial for the idea of 'Glenn James's patented brand of happiness' at this point. It all reeked of false advertising. "Do *you* know what's wrong with you?" Kitty smirked, facing her eggs once again. "Or are we still waiting for someone else to emerge?" She flung her gaze back up towards Glenn's open door before refocusing on her eggs. Beatrice laughed.

"Maybe someone a bit blonder?" Beatrice added. "Maybe someone with their clothes a bit more intact?"

"Oh leave the poor girl alone!" Hersey barked with desperate eyes that did battle against his angry brow. "*You*—" He focused on Kitty before widening the scope of his accusation. "The both of you can be so wicked, when does it end? Are you going to be cracking this wise at our poor Glenn's funeral?"

"She's not dead yet." Kitty muttered into her eggs. Beatrice mimed a silent apology to her father and Hersey's face softened, he turned back towards Glenn. There he stood and he begged, and he did so without moving a single lip.

A sparkle shined through from deep inside of Hersey James's eye. Decades of hurt that he had never been able to evoke, decades of hurt that went deeper than anyone could understand. Somehow, he showed that to Glenn. And Glenn, as only Glenn could, understood him completely. She closed her smile, seemingly happier now. Glenn took her last step down into the kitchen. She pointed her nose towards the ceiling for a moment and inhaled one sharp breath before coming back to face her family with softer eyes.

"What's going on?" Hersey cleared his throat before he spoke.

"Don't push her!" Kitty scolded. "Why should she talk to the man with the knife in her back? Tell me, Glenn. What could have possibly gone so wrong?"

Hersey laughed. "And why would she tell the one who hasn't shown any interest beyond the boy by her side?"

"Enough!" Glenn allowed anger to break her voice into a squeal. "I'll tell you when I'm ready, and I'll tell you all as one. I came out of my room, didn't I?" Glenn growled with frustration, she looked at Henry when she spoke, and the sounds quivered inside of the throat that ran dry. "If I can't be your sweetheart, if I've failed my casting, then I might as well accept my maternity." She straightened her back, worry shaded her face and her hair gleamed with darkness. "I, Glenn James; am pregnant with the spawn of Satan himself."

☙1979❧

"They know exactly what they're doing, Will." Hersey tilted his head back, squeezing a bottle of drops into his eye. "The worst part is that Elroy caught it all on camera. I'm sure the tabloids are gonna have something to say."

"You brought Elroy?" William—who had been inspecting Hersey's eyes in a lean over the counter—ejected himself away from his patient in disgust. "What could have possibly tricked you into thinking that was a good idea?" William yelled and the sound of his voice echoed all around the hotel bathroom.

"I thought I'd look like a hero." Hersey admitted. "Now either my daughters hate me, or I staged the whole thing for some controversy press. Wine's too sacred to be used as a weapon, it's the blood of Christ for God's sake—maybe that's the worst part of all this, the waste of a perfectly good glass of wine." Hersey blinked hard and his eyes dribbled solution from the drops.

"It's fifty-fifty." William added, ignoring Hersey's poetic wax about the wine. "Elroy can print whatever he wants. What're we gonna do about it, tell the truth?"

"Never." Hersey laughed a sarcastic kind of laugh. "She looked okay, though. She's fit for television if we can get her to come around."

"That's a surprise, her picture didn't exactly inspire confidence." William turned away from Hersey's eye to scan through the window. Glenn was splashing around in a hot-tub down by the courtyard, she spun in circles and spat hot water like a fountain to the other end of the tub. All the other children were gathering in the pool.

"A magazine is a lying thing, William. You taught me that." Hersey got up to join William in his gaze out the window.

"I thought you'd forgotten. What is Elroy but a liar?" William turned to Hersey. "He's attached himself to your hip, aren't you worried about what he might see? What he's already seen?"

"There's worse things to be than a liar." Hersey looked from the pool, up to his own reflection in the glass, and back down to the pool again. "I figured that one out for myself. You could be a liar, or you could be a nobody. Some people need to be liars in order to not be a nobody, and some people need to use those liars in order to not be a nobody." Hersey stared at Glenn now, the hot-tub's water turned to froth as she spun around and splashed circles around her body. "What imagination." Hersey muttered and smiled, though the sun's glare hurt his eyes and he flinched away.

"You don't think she was lying, do you?" William was still by the window while Hersey paced the room.

"Beatrice has always had a flair for overcomplications." Hersey squeezed his eyes shut. "And this is just about the most intricate plan I've ever seen. If her despair is a hoax, that is." He turned and paced to the other wall, then stopped. "I must say, she looked suspiciously healthy for someone who's supposed to be on a bender."

"She isn't a stranger to near death, though." William added. "Remember Jacksonville? Remember Madrid?"

"Very true." Hersey nodded and turned back once again. "But all of those were hoaxes in their own way. Maybe it's a boyfriend, maybe it's a gripe with me. The bottle's a vice like it is a tool, we both know that."

"Her antics have never gone so public before." William peeled himself away from the window to face Hersey while he spoke. "And *you* never felt the need to fly out before." William started to scold, but Hersey cut him off before he had the chance to work up to anything that was overtly accusatory.

"Like I said, some liars need to be used." Hersey opened his eyes, they were redder than ever.

"I was talking about Elroy." William frowned.

"Couldn't you have been talking about any one of us? Surely you're no saint." Hersey took a quick glance out the window. "Now, I'm off to take a dip." Hersey smiled and backed away from the window. "That's a *marvelous* game Glenn's playing out there. I can't miss out on all the fun up here with you." Hersey turned and left.

Alone in his room, William held his gaze out the window. He focused on Glenn, waiting for the moment when she'd see her father. William knew what was going to happen, he'd only seen it about a million times before when Glenn would visit the set—or later when she joined the show. He just wanted to see it one more time. He watched, Glenn splashed in a few more circles and pretended to fly an airplane around the perimeter of the hot-tub. She was so insular down there, so deeply entertained by her own mind. Then Hersey appeared, and her face exploded with joy.

"I can't believe we left!" Beatrice kicked her feet in the air to illustrate her exasperation. "I mean, who knows what he could be doing to Glenn. We've left her with him for way too long."

Still using the James family credit, Beatrice and Kitty were hiding out in style. The top-floor penthouse sweet of the Miller Inn to be exact. Waves crashed in the distance, Beatrice reclined in the sun that baked their balcony while Kitty flipped through an outdoor magazine on her bed. "You don't know her anymore." Kitty spoke but she didn't move her gaze from the page. "She's just like him. Ever since she joined the cast of that God forsaken show—she's beyond saving." Kitty flipped to the magazine's end.

"She would have never left us like that." Beatrice paused. "Do you think I'm going to end up with a raccoon's mask around my eyes?" She leaned around her seat so Kitty could get a look at her widely sun-glassed face.

"Take these." Kitty flung a pair of slimmer shades towards the door. "You don't think they'll be able to find us here, do you? I mean, with Elroy in cahoots with Hersey and everything, won't they know where to find us?"

"I hope they do!" Beatrice snapped her sunglasses off. Getting up from her seat to gather the pair that her sister had just flung, her tone intensified. "Then Glenn might have a chance to escape. We could bring her back to this quiet life with us!" The thought brought a smile to Beatrice's face.

"I'm telling you, she wouldn't go for it." Kitty got up from bed. Her tone, too, intensified. "She's her father, she's not us. She's an addict."

"*I'm* an addict!" Beatrice took a violent step towards her sister, she spat in Kitty's face when she talked. "I'm not dry, I'll never dry out completely. No matter how hard you stare and frown, no matter how much you shake your head and mope when I leave at night. I am them." Beatrice pointed towards the door. "And I know that you are too."

"I'm clean." Kitty backed up, exposing her palms to show their emptiness. "I'm no Beatrice James."

"Well Beatrice James is leaving!" Beatrice backed away from Kitty too. "If Glenn's too far gone, then I'm too far gone." She stopped in the doorframe, backlit by an intense yellow sheet of sun. "And I'm sorry, but I refuse to believe that." Beatrice's voice held so strong for most of her speech, she grinded words out through a tight stomach that refused something that was trying to show through. Still, she whimpered as she left.

Cameras huddled within the cracks of the lobby of the Miller Inn. Beatrice James emerged from the cover of the elevator's door, and they sprung out in an ambush. "*Aah!*" Beatrice jumped back in a moment of reactivity. She straightened up after a second or two, but that's when the questions started.

"Beatrice! How are you feeling?" Cameras flashed.

"Beatrice! You sure are a knockout for somebody with one foot in her grave. Tell the people, how do you do it?" Another camera flashed, this reporter snapped his fingers over the camera's lens in hopes that he might pull Beatrice's attention in that direction.

"Beatrice! Do you blame your father for a life like this?" That stopped her in her tracks, she couldn't ignore that one.

"A life like what?" Beatrice responded, she turned back towards the reporter with one foot out of the hotel's exit. She pivoted to look right into the camera's eye.

"*A life*—A life like yours." The reporter stammered. He was younger and smugger than most of the others in the room. He reeked of high education and he even stammered with confidence. Some of the cameramen lowered their cameras now, others kept on flashing away. "A life where you have to do all this for a headline." He swirled around the lobby with a wave of his hand, he smirked. "I mean, you can't enjoy having to suffer so much every time you want the world to remember that your name isn't *Gretchen*."

Beatrice almost screamed again. She staggered around in her spot on the edge of the lobby. Her face drained of all blood for a moment. She would have screamed at the reporter, she would have shattered the camera and called Kitty down to inflict some real rage; but the reporters had found their hiding place, and Beatrice recognized this one from Elroy's magazine. Beatrice took a deep breath. "What's your name?" She placed a hand on her chest, as if the pressure would be enough to slow her heart rate.

"Byron—" The reporter held his head high. "Byron Buxton." The sound of his own name brought a smile to his face, Beatrice imagined him repeating it in the mirror before bedtime as a child.

"Byron Buxton." Beatrice repeated. "Do you happen to know Elroy Bartholomew?" Beatrice stepped the rest of her body back into the lobby. She smiled to match the reporter, cameras flashed and she kept on smiling.

"I do." He was proud to say.

"Prove it to me." Beatrice's smile faded into skepticism. Seductive skepticism, if that's possible. "Take me to him."

William dragged himself to the pool. Pretending to read a Spanish newspaper, his eyes transfixed on his coworkers in the hot-tub. Hersey had Glenn in a spread-eagle above his head. He'd spin her around, count to three, then dip her into the hot water. Poor Glenn couldn't even get a breath in between her giggles.

Glenn's head was submerged in the water when William noticed Henry over in the pool. Had he been there the whole time? His black hair streaked behind his head and the water rippled like synchronized swimmers when he dove in. Ripples weren't the only thing swarming Henry in the water, just about every teenager in the hotel was clamoring for position nearby. Some tried to talk to him, some just treaded water—speechless. William kicked back in his chair, he dropped his paper and twisted his body to face his son. "Henry!" He called, and Henry, mid-dive, turned around as if he'd been caught in a felony.

Henry got out of the pool, the cloud of teenage girls followed him but he ignored their presence as he walked to his father's chair. "Dad?" He snapped a towel from the chair next to William, he dried his hair and a collective swoon erupted from the cloud behind him. "Are we shooting yet?"

"Why don't you go play in the hot-tub?" William folded the paper against his lap, he had never understood Spanish and the pictures weren't as much of a help as he thought they'd be.

"I'm not playing." Henry got very serious all of a sudden. He sat down on the chair next to his father, but he didn't relax. "It's called performance art."

Hersey panted when he got out of the hot-tub, he climbed the stairs and collapsed his hands onto his knees. "This game gets harder with each new daughter!" He smiled

towards William, who had seen the same game played with
Kitty and Beatrice before Glenn. Hersey held his back and
groaned when he sat down on William's other side.

Glenn fastened two hands together at the palms, she
placed them on top of her head and sank into the hot-
tub, swimming in circles with her hands sticking out like
a shark's fin. "I did a lot of thinking in there, playing with
a child is like time in the joint." Hersey laughed, leaning
over to William's chair. "Lots of opportunity for the mind
to wander." Hersey winked.

"And what's on your mind?" William started flipping
through his newspaper again, mostly just to find something
to do with his hands.

"Elroy." Hersey said the name like it was all a big
secret. "Elroy and that pesky camera of his." He smiled
and lifted his eyebrows until they got lost in the brim of
his beret.

The following conversation rose from whispers into excited
yells of victory that echoed throughout the pool deck. "To
room 900!" Hersey leapt from his chair, he brought his
fists above his head and struck a triumphant pose. He ran
off with a yelp and a chant that sounded like a duck call.

"Keep an eye on Glenn, will you?" William dragged
a few steps behind Hersey, he hung back and appointed
Henry as babysitter before following Hersey's mad dash
back to the body of the hotel. "Okay?" He turned back
around when Henry didn't respond.

"Okay!" Henry glared at his father the way some
teenagers do. He waited for Hersey and William to
disappear from his view in the courtyard, then he went
back into the pool.

"I'll distract him." Hersey walked and talked. "I'll walk in and offer him something exciting to write while you sneak around. Last I saw of him, the camera was in his bag. But I'll buy you as much time as you need to get in and out. With plenty of time for thievery in between, of course." Hersey ran up the stairs, he had rejuvenated since his play with Glenn, and William struggled to keep up.

Hersey had been waiting for multiple minutes by the time William reached the ninth floor of the hotel's stairwell. "Elevators exist for this exact reason!" William panted, but he was too tired to get mad, he was too tired for anything.

"Nonsense! This is a stealth mission, my friend." Hersey slapped William's back, William wheezed. "For all we know, the elevators could be packed with extended family members. Or worse, press. This mission should stay as small as possible." Hersey's sentence trailed into a whisper as the elevator opened its doors.

"*Ock*—Okay. Let's get this over with." William sucked air between his words, and he followed Hersey through the hallways.

Hersey knocked on the door to room 900, no response. He knocked again, a couple minutes passed in silence, still no response. Hersey turned his back towards the door. "Where could he be? The story's with us, why would he have left the hotel without us?" William shrugged, and the two of them turned back towards the stairwell.

They had to pass the elevator on their way, a bell rang and William turned towards Hersey. Sweat beaded on his forehead and he still spoke with a dry lump in his throat. "Stealth mission's canceled?" He darted a glance at the dreaded staircase and shivered.

"Consider it postponed." Hersey smiled, turned his shoulders, and joined William in waiting for the elevator. Hersey jabbed William's stomach because he knew that the air would squeeze out like a whoopie cushion, he fought his laughter when he proved to be right.

The elevator went down before coming up to the ninth floor, it stopped on just about every floor in between, too. It stopped at the eighth floor twice as long as any of the others and Hersey grew impatient, he stepped up before the elevator's dial reached the nine that was pasted on the wall. Nose-to-nose with the reflection that he cast against the elevator's door, Hersey gasped when it opened.

Massive eyes pressed against the other side of the door, swallowing Hersey's gaze as he stumbled back towards William. Big and brown, they beat down on Hersey in confusion. The nose that accompanied them was all but scraping against the door that pulled open.

"Where's Glenn?" The voice sounded remarkably *like* Glenn's. Hersey shook the shock from his vision—Beatrice. She looked through the tops of her eyes with a head that tilted forward. She held her gaze and only walked until she stood just on the other side of the elevator's door. She was as separate as physically possible.

"Where's Glenn?" Beatrice repeated, and Elroy walked out from behind her with a smile. He walked around to the back of the group and playfully shook William by his shoulders.

"Isn't this great?" He whispered to William from behind. "Beatrice James, back where she belongs!" He shook a little harder and William shoved him off.

"Glenn's with us." Hersey continued to back away from Beatrice. He wanted her to stay, but he wanted her to stay at a safe distance. "Glenn's *staying* with us."

Beatrice stepped forward in response, a smile came to her lips and her eyes fell down towards her hands. "You know, I've been thinking about that chat we had at the bar." She looked up, confident that a light would come to her father's face. It did.

"You have?" Hersey stopped his gradual retreat.

"Especially what you said about Glenn, about her being so worried and everything."

"She is." Hersey slid himself away from the window that led to the courtyard, away from the visible scene of Glenn in the hot-tub without a worry in the world. "She's tearing herself to shreds about it. I swear, she really is."

"I'll do it." Beatrice straightened herself up, she shook black locks away from her eyes and tilted her face towards the light of the hallway. She sucked her cheeks in and tightened her core. "I'll do it for Glenn." Beatrice sighed and Hersey smiled.

"The world will thank you." Hersey reached a hand onto the side of Beatrice's shoulder. To his surprise, she waited for a moment before pulling away.

Beatrice's breath rippled, she sighed with each new exhale and her head fell towards the floor.

"Stay clean between now and this evening." Hersey reversed course to push his way past Beatrice. He stepped into the elevator and turned around. "I'll rally the troops, meet me by the beach when the sun starts to set. I see this as a dinner scene, that means you have to look presentable." Hersey scanned Beatrice's body from top to bottom and back up again, her stomach fell and pitted against the bottom of her torso. She flexed her entire body and tried her best to return her father's smile. That's when the elevator's door closed.

Beatrice stared at the door as it slid shut in front of her, her lips clumped into a ball that she held to the side of her mouth, and she was still breathing in ripples. "You gonna be okay?" William patted Beatrice on the back as he made his way into the next elevator. She grunted, and that proved to be enough to ease William's worry. The door closed him out next.

It wasn't long before Beatrice's hands started to feel around in her pockets. She grasped at the green denim of her pants, and all around the contents of her clutch. Her face drained of blood, and it pulsed with an alien kind of blue when her name exploded from the mouth that waited behind her. "Beatrice!"

Beatrice jumped back to find a beam on Elroy's crazy-eyed face. "We did it!" He smiled, wrapping the slender girl into an uncomfortable hug.

"Now we can save Glenn!" Beatrice smiled, exhaling all the time.

"Of course, of course, after we have that little talk you promised." Elroy's eyes fluttered with expectation. "Trade's go two ways, young lady. I brought you back to Glenn, I held my end to the best of my ability."

Beatrice's smile faded as she followed Elroy in his limp back to room 900. He opened the dark door to a dark room, the floor was scattered with cameras and papers and pens that leaked ink into the carpet. Something about the mess intensified Beatrice's anxious thirst. "So there's something you wanted to get off your chest?" Elroy dug around his mess for a few seconds before emerging with a clean notepad in one hand and a pen in the other.

"Can I sit?" Beatrice motioned towards the foot of Elroy's bed, Elroy nodded and she cleared enough debris to take a seat. "All I said is that I'd be honest with you. Anything you want to ask—I'm here, I'm exclusive, and I'm ready to be honest." Beatrice eyed the mini-bar that sat above a pile of Elroy's clothes that piled in the corner of the room. Her mouth watered and her ears *buzzed* to deafen her to the sound of Elroy's voice.

"Beatrice?" She snapped out of it. "Did you hear me?" Elroy asked and Beatrice looked to the floor. "When did your battle with addiction begin?" Beatrice heard him this time, her gaze drifted back to the mini-bar, but she spoke as she stared this time.

"Since birth." Beatrice stood up from the bed, she walked to the mini-bar and poured one of the tiny brown liquor bottles into a glass.

"Didn't your father tell *you*—"

"He's doing the exact same thing in his room, you know. *'Rounding the troops'* as he says." Beatrice laughed, she dropped a block of ice into her whiskey glass and some of the liquid spilled out on the sides. "That's where I get my addictive personality from, you know? He gave me my first drink; I was Glenn's age, he was sauced and he thought of it as a kind of bonding experience, I suppose." Elroy flashed a picture, Beatrice didn't flinch.

"Does it hurt to see him?" Elroy gave Beatrice a sideways kind of look. "I mean, with all those *'deadbeat'* chants and all—did you think this would be your opportunity to finally get some remorse out of him?" Elroy flashed another picture of Beatrice, but his eyes were sincere when he lowered the camera away from his face.

"Remorse is a foreign language when your name is Hersey James." Beatrice chuckled, pausing to drop her gaze to her feet. "It hurts to see him, but it hurts to see Glenn more.

She's right there—at that age where he corrupts you, I mean." Beatrice took a generous sip from her glass, she coughed and twisted her face into a knot. "I was her age, Kitty was her age." Beatrice took another sip, coughed, and took another. "You're five or six or seven, and he gets to you." She spoke through the sting of the whiskey in her throat.

"What do you mean *gets to you?*" Elroy was viciously writing in his notepad by now, his hand swelled against his pencil and he stuck his tongue out at the corner of his mouth. "He doesn't—"

Beatrice cleared her throat, though she didn't respond. The sound was enough to wash the reporter's sour words from her air, though she said nothing more. Just turned her head in a kind of circular motion, neither a nod nor a shake. She looked to the side, and sighed. "He scans us, he speaks, or he doesn't speak, and one day he says something, or doesn't say something, and your whole world collapses in on itself." Beatrice finished her drink. "I don't know—"

"I know your father." Elroy scribbled in his notepad. He spoke clearly, though he didn't look up in the slightest. "I know what you mean." He tacked a period onto the end of whatever it was that he was writing, then he looked up. "Make me a drink?"

So she did, and she did again. Beatrice had always been an excellent bartender—being raised by Hersey James will do that to a person—and she had a knack for keeping the good times rolling once they had started.

Beatrice is also a bartender with one of the strongest pours on either side of the equator. It's the kind of pour that distorts both time and sound after the first couple of drinks. Six in, and both Beatrice and Elroy had fallen into a sleeplike state of drunken euphoria.

Beatrice was the first one to shake herself up to the sound of the bell, she sprang to her feet from her slumped position on the couch. She looked out the window, the sky was turning red and the sun was disappearing over the horizon. It was the bell of *The James Gang*, Hersey must've brought it from home. Beatrice shivered when she heard that ringing, it brought bad memories with it. The bell rang again and Elroy rolled around from his slump at the foot of his bed. "You're still here?" He groaned, his eyes followed the sound of the bell and he looked out the window.

"You're coming, aren't you?" Beatrice asked, her voice shook a bit and her question came from fear to turn it into a plea. She turned back towards Elroy from the window. The pit had reformed in her stomach, her head throbbed and she shielded her eyes from the glare of the sun. Elroy's hand shot a thumbs up over his head.

"My job is done." He spoke into the blankets that he was nesting into. "Definitely don't start any more drama down there, I think your family's given me more news than I can handle." Elroy laughed, though his speech was so muffled by the sheets that Beatrice didn't recognize his sarcasm until she was already well out of the room.

Beatrice fixed her hair in the mirrors of the elevator as it made its way down to the lobby of the hotel. She thought about Kitty as she looked at herself, between her tousled hair and the dark bags that formed under her eyes, she looked exactly like Kitty did when she was losing her grip on her emotions. Beatrice hated to look so wild, she straightened her hair with her nails and blinked the hangover out of her eyes. She shook the crust from her face, but the doors opened and nothing had changed.

The lobby had emptied of all extended family members. Beatrice didn't mind this so much, though, puke was just as likely as conversation if she tried to talk. Her footsteps echoed until the hotel floors turned into the beach's sand. The sun was hot on the coast, but the wind kicked off the ocean and cooled Beatrice's skin in waves that doused the heat whenever it got too intense.

Beatrice knew exactly where to go, though she found herself stumbling a great deal as the sand got deeper. A cloud of bodies swarmed just a hundred yards or so down the beach, the controlled chaos confirmed that it was a TV set. "*The James Gang… In Mexico! Pt.2*" An addition had been made to the first part's sign, it tickled Beatrice to know that this whole production was basically her doing.

"Ms. Beatrice James!" Hersey met Beatrice on her way to the set. Glenn stepped at Hersey's ankles and trotted as he walked. Glenn stirred, happy though invisibly restless. Her sight brought a smile to Beatrice's face, even if she was mimicking her father. "Can't you walk?" Hersey's smile faded. "What's wrong with you?" He knew *exactly* what was wrong with her, God knows he'd seen it plenty of times in his life. Beatrice stumbled up to them, she swayed in the wind for a moment before plopping herself into the sand in front of Glenn.

"Sweetheart." Beatrice smiled and placed a trembling hand on her sister's short shoulder. The wind blew straight across her face, the fresh air was doing wonders for Beatrice's dizziness. She swept the blowing hair away from Glenn's eyes and Glenn smiled at her sister. Beatrice saw three of Glenn—she was certain that this Southern sun was going to leave her a blind woman—but it didn't matter. Glenn trotted forward to hug her sister, but a tug at

Beatrice's collar sent her flying back to her father's height before she had a chance to receive it.

Staring Hersey in the face now, Beatrice missed the world as it was in the sand with Glenn. "One request." Hersey whispered so nobody could hear him on set. "One request." He repeated and jerked Beatrice across his chest by the neck of her shirt. They walked towards the set. "One request, one goddamn thing. That's all I asked!" Hersey half threw Beatrice into her seat at the set's fake beachside dining room table.

"Hersey and Glenn James, everybody!" The announcer started his spiel as he always did, even though this episode's only audience was a few crabs and a family that gathered half a mile down the beach. Hersey was distracted by Beatrice, he seethed while Glenn bounded onto the stage. *"Featuring Henry Elliot as Henry James, and Gretchen Williams as Gretchen James!"* The announcer continued. Gretchen and Henry waltzed onto stage and the opening theme started to play. Cheerful strings swelled, though the sound of Hersey's voice drowned that all into the background.

"You're lucky nobody can hear us right now." Hersey's gaze blinked towards the cameras before menacing back down to Beatrice. "You're lucky that the world hasn't seen you like *this*—that I won't *let* them see you like this." He paused, checking the cameras one more time, he seemed to rethink his phrase. "The world hasn't seen their rallying cry in primetime. The reason that they come together to *boo* those of us that can keep it together. I've shielded you from that kind of scrutiny since the day of Gretchen's casting. But the show must go on." Beatrice squirmed out of her seat.

"What do you mean?" She asked, scared and stumbling all around the beach.

"I'm done." Hersey lowered his voice as the show's intro wound down. "Sit down. I'm done protecting you, I'm done giving *them* something so abstract that they blame me for it." Hersey cleared his throat, smiled, and turned his head to the camera.

"In three... Two... One..." Beatrice's head snapped over to see that William was counting down on his fingers, he pointed towards Hersey as he whispered "Action."

"Welcome!" Hersey smiled into the camera, his voice calmed the rest of the way down and he folded his hands in front of his hips. "Now, I know you might have heard some concerning things about *The James Gang* recently." The camera zoomed out and Hersey placed a soft hand on Beatrice's shoulder. She sat in front of him and squirmed, but he held her in place and she smiled when she relented.

Beatrice waved into camera. Her movement was timid, but she smiled all the way through. The camera panned along with Hersey as he walked the length of the table, still speaking directly to the audience. "We understand your concern, and we appreciate *all* of you who have been looking out for our Beatrice." Hersey stopped his pace and broadened his smile. "So, here to ease worried minds and lift heavy hearts, I now present to you..." Hersey held his breath for a moment. "Beatrice James!"

Canned applause rained in from the speakers that rested just off to the side of the stage. Thunderous, robotic, sheets of applause that engulfed the sound in the camera more completely than a live studio audience ever could. Hersey sat down, and the applause quieted when Beatrice stood up to take his place in the camera's frame. Beatrice smiled and allowed the fake audience time to quiet its roar. "It's true." She affirmed with a nod. "While I appreciate all your support for me over the past few weeks, I am here to assure you that I am okay." Beatrice's smile widened and the applause started back up. Hersey stood up next to her, patting her on the back as he picked up the speech.

"Well isn't that just a relief to hear?" Hersey talked into the camera more than he talked to Beatrice. "Why do you think the people were so confused, Beatrice?" He turned his head, patted his daughter's back once again, and sat down for her to take the frame.

"Well, I'm glad that you mentioned that, dad." Beatrice never called her father 'dad'. The camera had flushed her cheeks and brightened her smile, it was as if an older version of Glenn had appeared when the camera started rolling. Kitty would have thrown up on the spot if she'd been there to see this, Beatrice knew that.

"I fell victim to a storm of bad luck." Beatrice sighed. "I went to Mexico for a relaxing beach vacation, but I got sick on the plane ride over! The very worst of my stomach virus was caught on camera, and that led the world into assuming the worst." Beatrice bit her bottom lip when she smiled. "An evil parasite was eating me from the inside out, but I'm happy to say that it's gone now." Her eyes blurred in and out of focus, the camera was the only place she found clarity. The camera, the one stagnant thing in a world that wobbled around her. "Beatrice James is safe." She said, without a hint of a shutter. She should have stammered, but she didn't. "Thank you for your concern, but there's no reason for alarm."

And she loved the camera, canned laughter ensued with rabid enthusiasm whenever Beatrice told a joke. The whole world stood in front of her eyes, and she didn't have to answer to a single voice on the other end. She was charming without being desperate, confident without overstepping. The camera was concrete and final and it felt closer to her than any human had ever gotten. Beatrice shed a tear before the end credits rolled.

"Wow!" Hersey reached down and shook his daughter by the shoulder. Canned cheers faded, and the episode's final shot cut to credits. He smiled without conditions, it was a smile that Beatrice hadn't remembered ever seeing before. "You're a true natural, my dear. You're a true member of *The James Gang*. Truer than I've ever seen!"

"Really?" Beatrice cringed as she spoke. She recognized the squealing weakness in her words as they came out, but her father smiled and laughed and she couldn't help but to follow his lead. She stood up and placed her hands on her stomach, she moved just as he did. Beatrice laughed at a joke she could never hope to understand.

Hersey sighed from laughing so hard, then he pulled Beatrice away from the group. Glenn tried to follow them, but Hersey told her to go play in the sand. Beatrice had forgotten all about Glenn since the episode ended. She was here to save Glenn, but what was so dangerous about all this? Beatrice turned away, eager to whisper with her father. "You should have been on this show the whole time!" Hersey hissed his excited whispers with wide eyes. "Where were you hiding?"

"Behind Gretchen, I suppose." Beatrice shrugged, but she laughed the comment off as if Gretchen was a thing of the past.

"Well you leave her in the dust! I swear, it takes a real James to be this dynamic. Sometimes I really wish I had cast all of you in the show from the beginning." Hersey motioned back towards the set where Glenn piled sand on top of the dinner table. "I mean, look how successful Glenn's become!" Hersey's smile was just as broad as it was free. He winked at Glenn when she looked up at him, and he stewed in happy silence when he looked back at Beatrice. "I'm seeing spin-off, I'm seeing the *'True'* James Gang all over this next decade." Hersey panted, though, despite his enthusiasm, Beatrice's attention had pulled away from the promises.

"What's wrong?" Hersey asked, holding tight to his disappointment. He tugged at Beatrice's arm, but her eyes had locked on something that approached from their hotel. Hersey looked, it was Elroy.

"Hello!" Elroy stumbled like Beatrice had before the camera sobered her up. He kicked clouds of sand as he stepped, and even his greeting was tinged with a hint of alarm.

Beatrice's heart-rate kicked into overdrive. Suddenly, she hated the idea that her father had known about her drinking. Drinking with Elroy was somehow worse. Her head throbbed, but Elroy smiled at Hersey and that diffused at least some of her concern. "*H*—Hersey, good man. You have made me a fortune!" Elroy reached out to shake Hersey's hand. Hersey shared a confused look with Beatrice, but he shook all the same.

Hersey piped up after a moment of awkward silence. "Would you like to fill me in on the details?" He asked, though Elroy wasn't going to accept silence for much longer, he could barely contain his excitement. He spat a stammered, slurring word before resetting his fading sense of composure.

"Pitching your family is a topic that sells itself! I just got off the phone with Mr. Wiggins, and he's seeing my vision." Elroy bit at his lips, he tried to contain his laugh but it wound up coming out in a single heave instead. He choked on his enthusiasm and took a moment to cough before moving on. "I'm seeing movies, I'm seeing reality programming, I'm seeing books and guest appearances! This goes *way* beyond television for you… This goes *way* beyond journalism for me!" Elroy bounced on his toes without ever fully leaving the ground. He bounced back and forth between Beatrice and Hersey's eyes, but he couldn't keep silent for long. "Let's celebrate!" He jerked back towards the town—and the bars—away from San Lucas Bay, but Hersey placed a hand on his shoulder.

"Stop." Hersey frowned and deepened his voice to a level of Kitty-esque bass. "We're here to celebrate one thing, and one thing only." Hersey released Elroy and wrapped that arm around Beatrice's shoulder, she blushed. "And that's the arrival of a new *force* in our kingdom of television!" He looked at Beatrice for a moment, then he turned back over towards Elroy. "This one's going to lead *The James Gang* into the 1980s, and beyond!" Finally, Hersey cracked a smile. He laughed, and pushed Elroy back towards the town.

Hersey insisted on passing up every bar that he saw—all of them that weren't Loomis's Spirits, that is. His face lit up when they finally saw the pirate ship-like shack after about two miles of coastal trekking. Beatrice had sobered the rest of the way up, something didn't feel right. She studied the joy that surrounded her, something was wrong and it brought the pit back into her stomach. *"Wait!"* Beatrice stopped the group just before they entered the bar, her voice cracked and remnants of her scream echoed around in the bar that she faced. Hersey turned around long before Elroy did.

"What's wrong, my dear?" Hersey heightened his own concern when he saw that Beatrice was looking at him as the subject of her scream.

Beatrice paused as she examined the look in her father's eyes. She liked the concern, she'd also diagnosed the reason for her stomach's pit. They'd left Glenn alone on the beach, poor baby Glenn was all alone with her pile of sand on the set that was never to be used again. Would she know her way back to the hotel? Was anybody there to help her find her way back to safety? Was the extended family truly to be trusted with something as sacred as the safety of a five year old?

Beatrice stopped her breath in the back of her throat. She watched while her father blinked, there was something like remorse in his eyes. Beatrice had never seen such remorse in her father's red eyes, not directed towards her, at least. "Nevermind." She waved her hand and blushed with a smile fit for television royalty.

Red wine mixed in with entire bottles of brandy inside the stomach of Hersey James. His eyes reddened with the flare of the wine, and they flushed into calmer tones with a rinse from the brandy. An old jukebox played new music in the corner of the room, "Moving in Stereo" played in the background, and Hersey zoned away from the room with a satisfied look on his face. A brandy in one hand, and a glass of wine in the other, he watched while his daughter danced with the younger people in the bar.

Spring breakers, no doubt. They were all vying for a chance to dance with Beatrice. They'd push and prod out there on the dance floor, dance had turned to warfare and it was all for a chance to get close to the one that Hersey saw himself in. Elroy talked—he always did—but Hersey was content to smile and drink and ignore.

Beatrice bounded back to the group after a few more Cars songs and a ballad by Kitty's close personal friend Barbara Streisand. Her exit sparked an array of groans from the young men that were left waiting in the wings. Dripping in sweat, she laughed at the sight of her father. "What?" Hersey preempted any speech that his daughter could muster. "What's with that lovely smile of yours?"

"It really is me, isn't it?" Beatrice yelled over the sound of the music that engulfed the interior of Loomis's Spirits. "You Make Loving Fun" by Fleetwood Mac. "I am the future of *The James Gang*." Beatrice smiled and sighed as she let her words sink in.

"I've known it all along!" Hersey yelled and Beatrice sat down beside him. He lowered his voice. "You're the bulldog that I am, you have something that Glenn could never learn—no matter how close she follows me."

"You mean it?" Beatrice leaned closer to her father, the song changed on the jukebox and she lowered her voice as the room became tame. "You're Kind" by Beatrice's close personal friend Paul Simon.

"Of course!" Hersey raised the volume right back up again. He yelled, and the bar's front door flung open. In all his volume, Hersey didn't notice the *thud* that came when the doors slammed nearby walls. "Glenn's America's sweetheart right now, I do mean that when I say it. But she's a bit part, and that's all she'll ever be. She's too nice, she's too agreeable, her charmed life has turned her into a flat character!" A hand tapped against the bone of Hersey's shoulder.

Hersey turned to see William. He held Glenn by the hand, and his facial features had all turned down. His hands were wet and he pulled Hersey up from his seat at the table. "Look who's coming to join us!" Hersey called back down to Beatrice and Elroy, but William was not in the mood for festivities. The table's nervous laughter died down, and Hersey turned back to his old friend.

"Do you know where I found her?" William still held Glenn's hand, though Glenn shrunk behind him. William gritted his teeth into an evil looking smile. Sweat beaded on his forehead, and his hair dripped in what must've been rain. Glenn's hair dripped too.

"Piling sand?" Hersey sounded so small in the face of William's questioning. He wouldn't look at Glenn, so he stared into William's eyes and allowed his own to water. "*Sh*—She was just on the set." Hersey started to stumble backwards, but William grabbed his sleeves and held him still.

"That was two hours ago!" William shook Hersey before dropping him back into his seat. Now standing above the cowering star, he *really* intimidated. "That was before the sun went down. It got *real* dark out there, Hersey! That was before she took to wandering around the coastline!" William jerked at Glenn's arm and Hersey flinched as if it were his own.

"*William*—" Hersey gasped, unable to move. Beatrice managed to pull Glenn away from his grasp, but other than that she had frozen.

"That was before *The Dilemma* got to her." William lowered his voice.

"*No*—" Hersey turned a wild eye towards Elroy, but William cut him off before he could scream.

"A camera flashed just as she was wandering into the surf. That's what caught my attention, but I got there too late." Hersey scanned over the two dripping bodies in silence. "Somewhere, there will be a picture of Glenn. Her father abandoned her, and the world's gonna have to see that eventually." William's anger turned into something mournful, he looked down from Hersey, and Hersey finally made eye-contact with Glenn. "I'm sorry Hersey, but I think we both know what this means."

Chester Wiggins was a stout military man. He made his fortune manufacturing bombs, planes and heavy weaponry. He kept a fleet of planes in the backyard of his upstate estate, and he could be around the world faster than anyone except the ghost of Howard Hughes. More recently, the old man had a crisis of conscience; after being held at gunpoint on his way to a performance of King Lear on Broadway, he switched his bullets in for a film camera and became the executive producer of *The James Gang*. His planes had been used for more pleasure than business in recent years, but they sure let him get to Mexico in a quick trip.

"You told him?" Hersey had become the one with the crazy look on his face. His cheeks turned green, almost seasick, and he clutched to the edge of the table for dear life.

"He's on his way, Hersey. He was going to find out eventually." William stank of shame, or pity. He shook his head and refused to raise his voice very much above a whisper.

"*N*—No." Hersey whispered too, but it was in a hoarse kind of way. "No, we can't go back to the hotel. We have to hide until this all blows over." Hersey's eyes darted from exit to exit, and he moved away from his seat. "We can save the show, we can salvage this—I *won't* give into this smear campaign!" Hersey lurched towards the front exit of the bar, but he ran into a brick wall in William's chest.

"Hersey, look around." William motioned back to the table where Beatrice and Elroy both toed the line between bewilderment and disgust. "It's over. There's nothing left of *The James Gang* to salvage." William grabbed Hersey's shoulder and smiled without showing his teeth.

"They would have printed Beatrice's story regardless." Elroy hung his head as if tabloid journalism was the eighth deadly sin. "Picture or no picture, there's more than enough to kill *The James Gang*. Beatrice gave me everything, and *The Dilemma* called before I got a hold of Mr. Wiggins." He sighed. "I could've taken it back, but the writing seems to be on the wall as far as the show's future is concerned."

"You're them!" Hersey turned, screaming the bar's music into silence. "You were them until you saw a check!"

"You had a good *ru*—" William started, but Hersey yanked himself away.

Hersey's voice lowered and his eyes darkened into shadows of themselves, he dipped his face away from the table. Hersey heaved on his breath, he arched his back and lurched in waves that sent him cowering to his knees.

Glenn was the one. She inched forward while the rest of the group leaned away, she ran over his back with a trace from her fingertips, she crouched down to his level. "Dad?" She tried him, she looked into his eyes but they only clamped into a tighter close. "Dad?" She tried again, though Hersey shook his head and buried his eyes into the palms of his hands. "Hersey?"

Finally, Hersey opened his eyes, tears leaked from both sides and he stumbled away from the table. His finger stretched in front of him, right towards Beatrice.

"Y—You..." His voice cracked and his finger shook. The rest of the table scrambled away from Hersey's point, and only Beatrice remained. "You didn't come here for Glenn. You came here for everything!"

Hersey regained his footing. "You don't drink to kill yourself, you drink to kill me! You didn't come for Glenn, you came because Glenn's absence is a poison! And to kill the show is to kill me too. You're *killing me*, Beatrice! Why did you talk to *him?*" Hersey lunged and motioned towards Elroy, then he keeled back over again. He held his stomach and continued with a groan. "When does it end, Beatrice? When does it end?"

"You're killing yourself, Hersey. The pictures don't have anything to do with me." Beatrice remained seated, she stared at her father and didn't blink. William and Elroy were both fading away from Hersey's finger, but Glenn hung around. "You drink and you lie, but you can do no wrong when you're blind to your own nose." Beatrice spoke slowly, just above a whisper. "You're killing yourself. And if I wasn't around to stop you, you'd kill Glenn too."

Hersey backed away as Beatrice spoke, he met her eyes and he backed himself all the way up to the bar. He waved a finger at the same bartender as the other day, nonverbally begging him for another glass of wine. "You're cut off." The bartender's voice boomed in a tone that startled the man who hadn't heard a '*no*' in almost a decade.

Hersey quaked for a moment, then he stood up and flattened a wrinkle that had formed in the breast of his raincoat. He turned, cleared his throat, and walked out the front door of Loomis's Spirits. He left with one phrase, one question to rattle the minds that he was leaving in the bar. "Wouldn't you?" He slammed the door, and Beatrice shivered with the echo of his exit.

"Beatrice?" Glenn poked at her sister. Beatrice had taken control of her father's wine, she was still sweating from her time on the dance floor, and her eyes glued to the door that shook to a close in front of her. "Beatrice?" She took his last sip, moving nothing but her arm and her lips to drink, she kept staring at the door.

"I'm him." Beatrice muttered. She swallowed the rest of her father's wine before switching over to his brandy. Her mouth gaped and she drank even as Glenn tried to hold the glass away from her mouth. "I'm cursed." She muttered as the brandy stung her throat. "The curse of *The James Gang.*"

That was the day Hersey James lost his heart.

ᔔ**1999**ᔕ

A casual ear would have probably called the police, or maybe even the fire department had they heard the shriek that ensued in the moments after Glenn's big announcement. It was a deep rumble of a scream, it washed the room into pin-droppable silence and hollowed Glenn's face out of any pride that had snuck in.

Kitty James stood up from her seat at the table, her eyes had seen a ghost and her mouth hung open in toothy terror. She pointed at Glenn as if the room needed a visual to know what it was that she was screaming about. It came in one sharp outburst. But the sound, and the echoing of the sound that followed and rang around the walls of the *James Gang* mansion, proved to be intractable.

Thankfully, for Kitty's sake, no outside passers by had been close enough to catch wind of the commotion that rang out from the walls of the kitchen that morning. Kitty's eyes lit up, and her nostrils flared with alarm. Her lips trembled, and the mere sight of her was enough to bring an intense heat to Beatrice's head. She sputtered her way through a word, trying to regain a face that was more safe to share as she spoke. "*W*—What?"

"You screamed." Beatrice answered from the side of her mouth.

"I know." Kitty scowled, embarrassed by her own outburst. Blood still boiled beneath the surface of her skin, her shoulders slouched, and she looked down in defeat. "I *just*—" Her eyes wilted into the surrender of a smile. "With who?"

Everybody, even Elroy, looked at Henry. The room fell silent besides the sound of the teeth that ground inside of Kitty's mouth. Her whole body clenched into stillness, yet she remained the loudest thing in the mansion.

Nico scampered across the kitchen floor, she was focused on a mouse that had reared its head out from a crack next to the front door in silence, even she knew who the father was. Henry smiled, he dodged the room with his eyes, and let them graze the floor to watch the cat. "It's me, Kitty." His mouth hung open, that last word, '*Kitty*', echoed around the kitchen and all throughout the ancient structure of the building. "I'm the father, we found out yesterday. It's me, not Satan." Henry looked back to Glenn, his face scolded her for the unfavorable comparison—even if he knew that she'd been referring to Hersey.

Kitty sat back and welded her eyelids shut to avoid falling over, her breath was thick and noisy as it raced in and out of her lungs. She was seeing herself from a far distance, like a camera that floated six feet above her head. She was a bystander in her own actions, and she watched herself hyperventilate. She squirmed in her seat, restless silence had taken over her voice and sealed her lips together. She watched from above while faces mired in confusion all around her.

"Well—" Hersey was the first to well up. He twisted his thumbs into loops around each other and he spoke like the words stung his throat. "How can you be so sure?" Redness surrounded the old man's eyes as he blubbered, though this redness seemed to pulse more than usual. He repelled from the soon-to-be parents with lips that quivered beneath his mustache.

"I got tested when I left yesterday." Glenn blushed.

"Is this what you were so upset about?" Hersey had lost all control over the volume of his voice.

"I didn't know how you all would react. I mean, I've spent so much of my life trying to keep this family together *and*—" Glenn rubbed her arm, pausing to glance at Beatrice, then to Kitty. "Well if this family's gonna tear itself apart anyway, then I suppose you won't care. It doesn't matter, I guess I went a bit mad there."

"You went mad when you did the damn thing!" Hersey looked at Glenn as if her ears had doubled in size. He checked with Beatrice who winced with the volume of her father's voice, he checked with Kitty who equalled his rage.

Kitty had long since finished her eggs. She stabbed at the remnants of food that scattered along the edges of her plate. Her hands were shaking and the fork *clanged* against the ceramic bowl like a bell that beckoned the neighborhood children home for dinner. *'Children'*, she never wanted to think of children again. With no more food left to be picked at, Kitty *had* to look up.

Beatrice measured a smile and hugged Glenn from the side before shaking hands with Henry. Secretly, she despised Henry for moving between James sisters like they were pegs on a ladder. Publicly, and with a mind for her future in acting, she held her tongue.

Hersey, with cheeks so red that they threatened to pop, commanded the room's attention as he spoke. "As the official spokesperson for *The James Gang*, I'd like to announce a death in the family!" Hersey raised his arms above his head and beamed with a false sense of pride that retracted Beatrice's hand from Henry's. "My child—" Hersey wrapped one arm around Glenn's shoulder, stepping her back onto the first step of the staircase. "I am vastly disappointed in you. My Glenn—perfect Glenn, America's sweetheart—you've died and come back as a parent!"

"*This*—This is what I was afraid of." Glenn choked on her words.

"Shouldn't you be happy for her?" Beatrice tempered the sound of the disgust in her voice. Something about the gesture was deeply artificial, but Glenn was glad to have an ally. "*The James Gang* will live on beyond you!" Beatrice forced a smile, though it seemed harder than usual to manage. She was gaining a quick respect for Glenn's ability to play both sides, to speak from both sides of her mouth.

"It's my fault." Henry stepped forward and hung his head from a string on his neck. "It was a mistake, I shouldn't have put her in a position that could sacrifice her future." Henry's voice yodeled with pain. He stared at Hersey with wounded eyes, and Hersey brought him into a hug.

"It's not your fault." Hersey whispered into Henry's ear. "It's not your fault." He glared at Glenn before ejecting from the embrace. He squared his shoulders in Glenn's direction. "Not everyone is meant to handle the power you have. Now, I doubt it—but I hope you chose wisely." Hersey sighed as if he were too tired to go on with such rage. He broke into a coughing fit that broke his stance, he crouched his hands onto his knees. The room dropped into silence and he staggered into the safety of the bathroom, clutching at both his stomach and his chest as he fled.

The day broke outside, the sun shone through gray clouds and dappled sunshine over the front yard of the *James Gang* mansion. Nico stomped through a flowerbed full of Camellias, endlessly proud of the dead mouse that hung between her fangs.

Henry sat alone on the front step of the mansion's entryway. He fixed his hair with one hand and twirled a cigarette around his fingers with the other. Sun lit the boy's face into a golden warmth, and he tilted his head up to stare directly into the rays that fell from above. He closed his eyes and blew out, covering the light with a thick sheet of smoke.

Just then, there was a cascade of feet stomping down from the staircase inside. The feet stampeded in a muffled rush that caused Henry to flinch and choke on the smoke that remained in his lungs. As he recovered from a brief fit of coughs, he stood up and reopened the door behind him.

"Henry, my boy!" Hersey smiled from the top of the staircase that led down to the basement. "We thought you'd disappeared!"

"What're you up to?" Henry asked suspiciously. He walked back through the door, slithering a smile onto his lips as he craned his neck in an assortment of directions to try to see beyond Hersey's body and into the basement that he guarded.

"Oh, well don't think it's a secret!" Hersey exclaimed. He stepped to his side when he noticed the inquisitive look that snuck onto Henry's tanned face. Henry passed the old man's welcoming hand, and the old hand corralled him down the stairs and into the deeper caverns of the basement. Henry checked back to make sure that Hersey was still there, the old man reassured him with a smile and a yell. "I don't blame you, my boy." Pain reentered Hersey's voice as his mind crawled back to Glenn. He looked down to his boat shoes, but his smile remained.

Hersey and Henry turned the corner together, an intense light shone on the two men from the main room. Henry flinched as his eyes adjusted and Hersey stepped in front of him, not missing a step. "We're back!" Hersey extended yet another unveiling arm, this time he framed a table that sat in the middle of the basement. There, Elroy and Beatrice sat and waved with intense hospitality in their eyes. Henry cautioned each foot as he stepped up to the table. The room was palpable with excitement.

"Mind if I have a seat?" Henry asked, still cautious as he pulled two empty seats out from the table. He extended one towards Hersey, and slowly lowered himself into the other.

Elroy was the first to speak, and he yelled his words with a voice that squeaked. "The great Henry Elliott is always welcome at our table!" The old man smiled with rotting teeth that separated from each other and soured the smell of his breath. Henry recoiled, but Elroy misunderstood his reasoning. "*Oh—*" He stuck a comforting hand to Henry's chest. "We're just decompressing from all the discomfort of this morning." Elroy smiled. "As you can see, the incendiaries are far from this table."

"You mean Glenn." Henry folded his fingers into a tent around his mouth.

"And Kitty, nothing will shatter when you stick with us!" Elroy patted Henry on the chest, his voice *cooed*, but resentment came through. "We were actually hoping to speak with you, so we really are lucky that you're here." Elroy paused, forming each sentence as he spoke the one prior to it, he had caught up to himself.

"Go on." Henry encouraged, he leaned his elbows onto the rickety table. His stomach was sick, but his intrigue got the best of him.

"You are Henry Elliott…"

"Of course I am."

"How would you like to make a return to the character of Henry James?" Elroy smiled. The resentment left his words and he removed his hand from Henry's chest in anticipation.

Henry's eyes grew wide as his smile became more confident. He scanned the faces that surrounded him at the table, searching for any clue that alluded to some kind of sick, practical joke. "*Are you*—Surely you're not serious?" He leaned even more of his weight over the table, focusing on Elroy while remaining keenly aware of the expressions of the other members of the group.

"Serious." Beatrice smiled without using her teeth. She clutched Henry's wrist. She was serious, Henry could always tell when she was being serious.

"Oh my God." Henry relaxed the caution that clenched in his face, he stood up and repeated himself to the entirety of the Eastern United States. "*Oh my God!*"

All that sound came out as a dull thumping to the Jameses that were left upstairs. Kitty and Glenn sat through the verbal earthquake, knee-to-knee, across the corner of the kitchen table. Neither of them spoke for what seemed like an eternity, Kitty kept licking her lips and Glenn kept touching her stomach. Glenn stared at Kitty, unblinking in her seat while Kitty looked in every other possible direction. "Why aren't you happy?" Glenn finally asked.

"In general?" Kitty looked up, slouching over the table and propping her head up with a hand. "I'm not quite sure, actually." Dismissing the question, Kitty stood up and looked out the window that had a view of the backyard. Nico pawed at a Camellia, Kitty turned her back towards Glenn.

"You know what I mean. I sure could use *somebody* in my corner for all this." Glenn stood up and followed her sister to the window. "What're you looking at?"

"I think you know why I'm unhappy, and I think you're asking for me to forgive you." Kitty looked at Glenn for a moment of silence. "You know I loved him more than you ever could." She blinked, and tears obscured her vision as the garden morphed into an amorphous blob of green. Glenn cleared her throat but offered nothing in response. "The winter flowers are dying."

"Of course they are." Glenn rubbed her stomach with both of her hands. She massaged her lack of a bump, searching for something to hold onto while she peered out the same window. "Some things have to die for more beauty to take their place."

"Now there's a depressing thought."

"What?" Glenn squinted at her sister. They both turned back to face each other, and Kitty glanced down at her sister's stomach.

"How old are you?" Kitty surprised Glenn with the question. "How old are you?" She repeated.

"*I—*" Glenn stammered before reapplying her sense of assuredness. "Twenty-five, why do you ask?"

"Because you've gone and turned yourself into a winter flower, and the worst part is that you're *smiling* about it!" Kitty sneered. "What, you're preparing yourself for your death? You're wilting in the sun already? My dear, you've hardly begun to live!" Kitty backed off. Red in the face, her eyes calmed down and drifted towards the staircase that went to the mansion's highest floor. "I just hope you're not doing this for *his* attention." Kitty quieted her voice as she drifted away. Her feet followed her drifting gaze. "His attention is suicide, you should have learned that by now."

"It's the wrong kind of attention."

"Any attention is enough for you and Beatrice."

"Don't you drink anymore?" Glenn yelled, still in the kitchen as Kitty climbed the stairs.

"What, are you asking if I'm drunk?"

"No, of course not. I just need something to do with my hands—a cocktail, perhaps? What would you like?" Glenn searched for a cocktail glass before bending over to search through the liquor cabinet that hadn't been touched in years. "We've got everything you could think of!" Glenn yelled again, and Kitty stopped her drift up the stairs.

"I stopped drinking when Beatrice got sober."

"More for me." Glenn murmured into the cabinet, pulling out the vodka and mixing it with some tonic from the fridge.

"What're you doing?" Kitty ran back down the stairs with wild eyes and a frown on her face. She pulled the glass from her sister's grasp and repeated herself. "What *do* you think you're doing?"

"Getting it over with!" Glenn cried and her eyes bulged out.

"Getting what over with?"

"The damage!" Glenn was *not* murmuring now. "Can you blame me for being proactive about it?" She ripped the glass back from Kitty as she yelled. Her eyes glowed in hints of black that matched the girl's new hair. She looked as she did when she first re-emerged from her bedroom. Feral.

"*Surely*—" Kitty searched for her words. "Surely you can't expect me to know what you're talking about."

"You should know better than any of us!" Glenn's steady increase of emotion erupted into a scream, and she smashed her glass against the kitchen floor. "The pain you inflict can only match the pain you feel. You're hanging on by a thread, Kitty. Everyone can see it." Kitty turned away as her sister reached out for her hand.

"I still don't see why that should make you go and poison your child."

"Is that as cruel as bringing another vulnerable soul into this family? This family that turns its back on you when your cute face has aged, this family that drinks and degrades its daughters for the sole sake of ego, this family that cannot even be called a family unless *The Daily Dilemma* is asking? And Henry, he's already a James. I can see our father in his eyes, soon they'll burn and sting just like his. That perpetual cry comes when you realize that you're too old to atone for the sins of your past. He tries and he fails. I know Henry will fail all the same."

"Is that why you think he got mad at you?" Kitty's deep voice quieted. "Because a child is a marker that you've been aging?"

Glenn sniffled. "I've ruined his delusion. I've realized why I was dispensable to the new version of the show, it's not because of a kid or Beatrice or anybody. It's because, no matter how hard I've tried, he doesn't see that little girl anymore." Glenn shrank, looking at the floor instead of Kitty. "The kid's an excuse. We've always been that, '*excuses*' for him to use as justification."

Glenn's eyes sank, and her head fell towards her feet. Kitty couldn't see her sister's eyes anymore, but she could tell that she cried through the sound of her voice. "Kitty, please make the room stop its spinning!"

"Let's go to the roof." Kitty suggested, and Glenn collapsed into her arms as she grunted in the affirmative. "Let's get some air."

"I have a lot to live for, you know." Glenn spoke in between deep inhalations as she got comfortable on the roof that was accessible through the window of Kitty's room. She looked into the sun and spoke with open ends in her words, seeking some kind of affirmation to close each syllable for her.

"Of course you do." Kitty forced a smile and placed a hand on Glenn's knee. "That's not what I meant. I guess I was projecting with all that talk about attention. People like Henry and Hersey—their attention is a ray of sun at the bottom of the ocean, when it shifts the ocean gets so dark that you—*you want to...*"

"You want to kill yourself?"

"I want to kill *something!*" Kitty buried her head into her hands and dropped her hands in between her knees. "*Will you*—Would you kill me?"

Downstairs, the table was filled with bug-eyes that leaned on hands and stared intently towards the man that stood at the head of the congregation. "I just want you to know..." Hersey smiled, heavy breathing provided an excited undercurrent to each word that he spoke. "That no matter how far off my travels may take me, how many people I get to see and how much of the world I get to experience..." He paused, smiling at each member of the table with twitchy-eyed nostalgia. "I will always find my home inside the arms of the ones I love the most... My family."

"Bravo!" Elroy exploded from his seat and started an infectious wave of applause.

"I really can't believe that you remember that old speech." Henry said. "You've been waiting a long time for this moment, haven't you?"

"Well, I'm an old man with a lot of time on his hands. Old lines are good to keep the brain sharp." Hersey knocked against the side of his head with a playful fist.

"We should all try one!" Beatrice joined in, uncharacteristic in both her excitement and her candor. "A big scene that includes all of us. It'll be just like the new show! How about the test scene from the first episode, surely you all remember that one." Beatrice smiled and focused in on her father.

"Well, okay." The old man's rhythm slowed and he lowered himself into his chair before noticing that everyone else had stood up. He followed their lead.

"What can I say? The kid in front of me kept holding his test up to the light. It was like he wanted me to cheat!" Henry raised his voice to match the prepubescent tone of his past.

"You got in trouble because you broke the rules, I think you should tell Mr. James before he finds out from the principal!" Beatrice joined in, cartoonish, amateur in her acting.

"*What was*—What was that?" Hersey stumbled over his words. He mimed an entrance to go along with the line, though his mouth drooped when he finished speaking.

"Oh no!" Beatrice and Henry exclaimed in unison, they smiled into each other's eyes while they groaned. "It's Mr. James!"

"That it is." Hersey twitched his face into a shaky smile, he squirmed and shut his eyes into creases of a hundred little folds. "Now, what was this I heard about cheating?"

"I'm sorry." Henry sighed, puppy-dog voice and all. "I cheated on the big test."

"*Weh*—Well I'm proud of you for telling the truth about it." Hersey brought his hand up to wipe sweat from his forehead. His face winced into a smile and he focused all his remaining strength into his core.

"Are you okay Mr. James?" Henry reached a hand out and put it on Hersey's elbow, it was cold and trembling, covered in moisture.

"Now, I want you to apologize to *you*—your teacher tomorrow." Hersey fell into his chair, still in character.

"Call an ambulance!" Elroy yelled and pushed Henry, the movement coaxed both him and Beatrice into high alert.

"You, you kids, you kids sure know how to keep me on my toes." Hersey continued his lines, though his eyes were glazing over and his head was reaching back past the edge of his seat. "I love you all." Hersey convulsed. Once, two times, before closing his eyes and seeing in black.

Glenn and Kitty were standing side-by-side on the very edge of the roof when they saw the ambulances pulling into the mansion's massive parking lot. One pulled in between the Jaguar XJS and the Dodge Challenger, and the other one blocked them in. Both Glenn and Kitty had been inching towards the roof's end in trepidatious, anguished, solidarity. Both Glenn and Kitty stopped in their tearful march when they heard the sound of the sirens.

A stretcher rolled in, it was being carried by four very serious looking people with white uniforms and clenched jaws to match the urgency that they carried in their stride. They disappeared into the front door of the mansion. "What was that?" Kitty asked the air as much as she asked Glenn.

"You don't think they're coming for us, do you?" Glenn added a question to the top of Kitty's. They shivered in the breeze that formed at such a high height. "That would be the cops, right?"

"Nobody noticed us." Kitty tilted her head over the side of the roof, she lost her balance in a gust of wind for a moment before leaning back onto her heels. Ghostly, her eyes lit up in line with the sound of the front door's reopening.

There, Hersey laid underneath them, green in the face and prostrate across the stretcher. The four jaw-clenching men rushed the shriveling old man into the back of the closest ambulance. They were gone as fast as they had arrived. "Still wanna kill yourself?" Kitty turned her attention back towards Glenn—who had turned a shade of green that almost resembled her father. Glenn breathed heavily, she stared at the ambulance until it disappeared into the distance, then she sprinted back in through the window to Kitty's room.

"What's happened?" Glenn yelled as she met Henry and the others in the mansion's front room. She panted, only stopping her sprint after flinging herself into Henry's arms.

"Where did you run off to?" Henry asked, gently tilting the mother of his child back onto her feet. "And where's Kitty?" Just then, Kitty emerged from the doorway that led to her room, she took a deep breath before joining the rest of the group in the foyer. There, they put on shoes and overcoats, hats and scarves, all the best to see a man who may not be alive to care.

"I'll drive!" Henry brandished his keys and extended his arm into the air. Glenn spoke, but her words were lost in the fervor. Henry began to run, leading the pack to the green BMW that was parked along the edge of the mansion's expansive driveway. "Everybody pack in!" He opened the door and barked his direction in a tone that reminded the girls of their father. Glenn sat in the passenger's seat while Kitty, Beatrice, and Elroy, slotted into the claustrophobic back seat like sardines in a can.

"Can *somebody* tell me what's going on?" Glenn yelled and pivoted towards the three that sat in the back seat. Elroy was the first to regain his composure, he was also the next to speak.

"We were reciting lines." Elroy's words chopped inside of his throat and came out in sudden jolts of sound. "*It*—He seemed to be having fun. He was smiling." Elroy swallowed hard and looked towards both Beatrice and Henry before continuing. "But he fell, he fell and his head fell back in his seat. He turned green."

"And then what happened?" Kitty chimed in, asking the question mere milliseconds before Glenn could open her mouth.

"He fell!" Henry yelled and slammed his hands into the steering wheel. "Didn't you see him down there? He was green so we called the ambulance, end of story." Henry spoke with great frustration. He glared at the road and accelerated to turn the car's engine into a low growl.

"Is he sick? Did he have a heart attack? A stroke?"

"Goddamnit Glenn!" Henry's face grew hot and red. "I don't know what happened to the old man and we're all just as scared as you!" Henry forced a whisper of his smile onto the end of his tantrum. There was defeat in his eyes, like a baby that was forced to watch while their candy disappeared from their grasp. He had felt the next iteration of *The James Gang*, and it was slipping through his fingers.

Henry leaned on the accelerator, the bodies in the backseat tossed from side to side with each turn, and Glenn grabbed hold of every handle that she could find near the passenger's seat. She braced for an impact that seemed inevitable.

Luckily, no impact. Not until they reached the hospital's parking lot, at least. The BMW screeched past the urgent care, took a sharp right around the hospice center, and rammed to a stop on a curb that served as a walkway to the ICU. "Good aim!" Beatrice exclaimed in a tone that bordered on sarcasm. Henry laughed, though nobody waited around to decipher her meaning. Instead, they raced through the front door of the ICU, and demanded Hersey James.

"From the old TV show?" A portly nurse with knotted hair stared at the group, she had lights in her eyes and she seemed to be squatting behind the front desk of the ICU. "*Oh*—Yes, I'm sorry." She took a moment before snapping back into work mode, though she had more than a little help from Beatrice's stink eye.

The nurse typed for a moment of breathless silence. She scanned over a list on her cinderblock of a computer, she mouthed the sounds of names over and over again until, "Hersey James! Looks like he's in room 70." She spoke and the group sprang into action.

Glenn and Kitty led the group in tandem, their long legs syncopated and tore through the hallways with indignant concern to carry each step. Beatrice, Henry, and Elroy, all followed suit, they read each room number with such echoing anxiety that the hallways filled with the sound of their quivering countdown. "77... 76... 75..." All ten legs sped up, they kicked at the air and squeaked against the polish of the hospital floor. Then they stopped. "70." Henry reached for the door, but his hand met Kitty's in place of the handle.

"Wait." Kitty and Glenn spoke in unison. Beatrice stepped up to the front, orienting herself next to her sisters and nodding in agreement. "We should be the first to see him."

Henry pulled his hand back and slotted it into the pocket of his corduroy pants, he looked up to see the three girls in a line. Only then did he realize just how similar they all looked. "Maybe this is a family after all." He said with eyes that drifted towards and ultimately landed on Glenn. "Be my guest." Henry bowed, he took a step away from the door and raised his hands up past his ears as a gracious white flag. Kitty was first the one to reach out, she caught the handle and turned.

"Ready?" Kitty twisted back around to face her sisters before opening the door. Glenn's eyes had filled with tears, but constant sniffling seemed to keep them at bay. Beatrice closed her eyes and focused on her breathing. Slowly, her nostrils expanded for deep inhales, and her lips parted for long exhales.

"*Ready.*" Glenn said with shakes in her voice. She sniffled once more. "Ready." She said, more concrete this time. They both looked to Beatrice, the hardened one, the one that had always shut her eyes from the pain.

"Ready." Beatrice opened her eyes, they darted from Kitty to Glenn, and back to Kitty again. She winced at the sight of something in Kitty's face, and her eyebrows formed the shape of a pyramid in the center of her forehead. "I'm sorry I abandoned you." She turned from Kitty, back to Glenn. "And Glenn, I'm sorry I tried to replace you too." Glenn smiled at her sister, and Kitty opened the door.

The door swung open to unveil a room that was saturated by the sun. The old man lay golden in his hospital bed, his pale face served as a perfect blank canvas for the sun to paint upon. He groaned along with the entrance of his daughters. Unable, or unwilling to turn his head, he asked "Who goes there?" His question came in the form of a grunt, and he clutched at his stomach as soon as it let go of his words.

"It's us." Glenn said gently, walking with soft feet as she led her sister's approach to their father's bed. "What's wrong, dad?"

"I'm dying! Next question."

"Okay, dad." Beatrice was next to approach, she rested a gentle hand on her father's shoulder and smiled at him. He flinched at the sight of her.

"What're *you* doing here?" He barked and writhed around on his bed. Speech seemed to be the cause of great pain. "There isn't a camera in sight, no publicity to be gained here. You can go home now!" Hersey waited for a moment, gargling his breath and regaining some of his strength. *"All of you!"* Suddenly, Hersey rolled over onto his side. He flailed his arm into the air and shrugged Beatrice's hand away from his shoulder.

"We're not going to leave, Hersey." Kitty said. "We're concerned about you and we have every right to be." She folded her arms and leaned against one of the many blank cabinets that decorated the room.

"What right? You're no daughter of mine!" Hersey winced, but he had to yell. "Only Glenn was a daughter of mine, and I cast her aside like she didn't mean a thing." The old man rolled over once more. "She changed, corrupted herself, and I cast her aside." He groaned even louder as he lifted his head to face his three daughters. "Now go!" He barked, familiarity rang out in his gruffness.

"Dad—"

"I mean it!" Hersey James strained his voice and grabbed at his sheets, white-knuckled in pain. "*Get out!*" He screamed at the girls, his girls, his lips shook to match the shaking tears that dripped from the corners of Glenn and Beatrice's eyes. All three of them jumped when they heard the rage, the self-pity, and the resentment that poured from their father's pained lips.

Kitty was the first to leave. It was a simple turn and exit for the one in the brown, the one in the overalls, the one that saw the rage on her father's face and drew upon decades of remembered resentment. She closed the door behind her, and Beatrice flinched in that direction.

Beatrice was next, though she hesitated a great deal. She turned back towards her father a few times on her way out the door. She swung her jet-black hair as she turned, hopeful to catch a glimpse of that newfound redemption in her father's eyes. Her lips turned down and she shut her eyes back into meditative slits as she exited the room in a storm of *clomping* footsteps.

Glenn lingered longer than either of her sisters. She watched while Kitty took her father's command and she even held Beatrice's hand as she turned away from the deathbed. The same deathbed that Glenn couldn't stop staring at, the same deathbed that housed the small man that had once represented everything that felt so big in her life.

"Do you still love me? Like you used to, I mean." Hersey asked in a voice that shrank as he spoke. Glenn brushed black hair from her face, and she watched her father turn over once again. She caught a glimpse of her own new look out of the top of her eye, and she hated it. All of a sudden, she yearned for the blonde, for the things that brought light into her father's eyes. She longed for the times when she was naive enough to see her father's love as unconditional.

Red washed Glenn's face with guilt. She yearned for her smile to come back, so she forced one onto her lips. She smiled at her father's back as he questioned her from his bed. It was not the same.

"Of course I do." It could never be the same again. Glenn allowed a breath to sputter past her lips, only then did she realize that she had been holding her breath since she stepped into the room. Glenn bowed her head to her father's unmoving body, she placed a hand on top of her stomach, and she started to exit the room.

"*Wait!*" Hersey turned to face the last of his daughters, and he used the last of the breath in his lungs. He waited to see Glenn's eyes, then he cast his own down to her feet. "You know, I never meant for you to have to pick between me and them." His voice was shrill, he was running out of strength to talk.

"I know, dad." Glenn smiled, lying.

"I didn't mean for any of this to happen. I loved you, but I was never meant to be a father to anyone."

"You were a father to me." Glenn smiled again. This time, she didn't lie.

"And you were a father to us all." Now, Hersey smiled too. "I don't know when this happened, maybe it's always been this way, but you became some sort of glue for our dysfunction. I know how tiring that can be, Glenn. You were the only one to ever play both sides of *The James Gang*, it's a hard job to be a mediator." Hersey's eyes were dripping like twin leaky faucets by now, his gaze dropped to Glenn's belly and his voice cracked. Glenn cried, but Hersey's smile widened and he met Glenn's eyes when she whimpered. "Now you won't have to." Hersey winked. "Get out!"

"Did you get to him?" Beatrice asked Glenn as she drifted into the hall to join her sisters. Elroy and Henry had both gone off to find a nurse, demanding answers that no longer mattered. Glenn released her belly to grab Beatrice's hand.

"You know him." Glenn said. She couldn't help but to laugh a little bit. "Stubborn as ever."

"Oh." Kitty sighed from her position, leaned up against another wall. Her posture didn't care, but her words couldn't hide from Glenn. Beatrice's face twitched, and Glenn noticed the same kind of stubbornness that she had just left in the other room. This too brought a reluctant smile to Glenn's face. Her oldest sister began to object.

"Surely you can convince him to fight this, or at least have him answer a few questions! You were always his favorite, Glenn. He would do anything for—" Glenn raised her hand up near Beatrice's mouth, she placed the other one on her stomach and allowed her voice to crack as she spoke.

"This world isn't for him anymore." Glenn said. She closed her mouth when she was done speaking. No open syllables, no room for argument. An aura of her former sage wisdom surrounded Glenn once again. She glowed through her surface-level change and conjured a warmth that coaxed even Kitty away from the wall. Glenn lowered her hand, and the three girls sat down in the chairs across the hall. The chairs were maroon with a hideously neon orange trim, the three girls cringed as one.

"Is this for the best?" Glenn asked out of seemingly thin air.

"What do you mean?" Beatrice leaned back to allow Kitty to see across her lap.

"Is this the best thing for us? To let go of him?"

"To let go..." Kitty repeated Glenn's sentiment in a softer, more ponderous tone. "I'm surprised to hear you saying that, he always liked you the best."

"Exactly!" Glenn leaned forward and injected more life into her voice. "And I loved him all the same, but that doesn't absolve the fact that I spent my past twenty-five years in competition with the ones that I should have been leaning on!" Glenn sighed and looked at the ground for a moment before setting her gaze back on to her sisters. "That's not the world I want to live in, our father's world of competition for love." Glenn patted her stomach. "I know that we all have our moments. We are only Jameses, after all. But his world was no world for us to grow up in, his world was no world for a little girl."

Glenn paused and her attention gravitated to the life that brewed in her stomach. For the first time in her young life, she sat comfortably in silence. She inhaled a deep breath and held it in to savor every moment with the air in her lungs. She couldn't help the smile that appeared on her face.

"So..." Kitty leaned over Beatrice's lap and cracked a smile to match the one that had taken control of Glenn's face. "It's a girl?"

Glenn didn't answer, just kept on smiling. And just then, a sound clicked on in the top corner of the hallway where a small, oddly-placed television was mounted on the wall. The color was grainy and the canned laughter was incessant, there was a young man smiling and comforting his three children on a golden-rod couch that sat in the middle of a uniquely seventies-looking family room.

Henry Elliott appeared into the hallway with Elroy on his hip, and both of the boys were immediately entranced by the goings on inside of this strange television. "I loved this scene." Henry said, and a wisp of a smile attached to his lips. On screen, Hersey James rubbed Glenn's small head and smiled into her eyes. He looked up into the camera. "I love you kids more than anything in the world." He said. Roll credits.

That was the day Hersey James lost his body.

CPSIA information can be obtained
at www.ICGtesting.com
Printed in the USA
LVHW041244090623
749280LV00002B/291